A MESSAGE FROM CHICKEN HOUSE

If you put a toe in the water with THE DROWNING then Rachel Ward's stunning sequel takes what happens next on to new depths of scary emotion! More intense, more about relationships and with an even more disturbing evil in the water, this is a thriller that will keep you on the beach and out of the pool all year long! But more importantly I love the way Rachel makes those voices in your head come alive – you know, the ones that we think are the 'real us', comforting, commenting and encouraging. But can you trust what they are saying?

BARRY CUNNINGHAM
Publisher
Chicken House

WATER BORN
RACHEL WARD

2 Palmer Street, Frome, Somerset BA11 1DS

Text © Rachel Ward 2014

First published in Great Britain in 2014
The Chicken House
2 Palmer Street
Frome, Somerset, BA11 1DS
United Kingdom
www.doublecluck.com

Cover and interior design by Steve Wells
Cover photograph © Yolande de Kort/Trevillion Images
Typeset by Dorchester Typesetting Group Ltd
Printed and bound in Great Britain by CPI Group (UK) Ltd, Croydon, CR0 4YY

The paper used in this Chicken House book is made from wood grown in
sustainable forests.

1 3 5 7 9 10 8 6 4 2

British Library Cataloguing in Publication data available.

PB ISBN 978-1-909489-32-5
eISBN 978-1-909489-59-2

This book is for the people who inspired me while I was writing it:

Ozzy, Ali and Pete — the 'usual suspects'.

My Mum and Dad.

The staff and students at Pontypridd High School.

And Matthew Evans, who has shown me, in a wonderful way, that you really can be the author of your own story.

Prologue

Water Born

You need eyes in the back of your head with kids, don't you? They're there one minute, gone the next.

Someone nearby shouts and it brings me back to my senses. I look around and she's not next to me. Nicola. I can't work out where she is, but she can't be far away. I only took my eyes off her for a second, didn't I?

Then I see her. See what people are shouting about. My granddaughter. A little black dot on the ice. She turns round and waves. And that's when it gives way. The ice. And she's gone.

I scream, along with everyone else, but I can't move. I can't *move*. A few metres away a young man launches himself on to the lake. He skids with long steps for the first part, then slows, stops, looks. Listens. He lowers himself down, flat on his stomach, and elbows his way towards the gaping hole.

My heart's in my mouth as I watch. He leans over, in, his legs sprawled on the surface, his head, arms and chest underneath, like he's been cut in half. And then he slides forward. An inch. More. Faster. And he slips underwater.

There are louder screams from the bank, but mine isn't one of them. I'm silent now. Struck dumb as I picture him and her, their faces underwater, their limbs thrashing.

Not again. It can't happen again.

And then a hand grips the edge of the ice.

The young man levers himself up a little way and lifts a small, dark bundle on to the shelf. He pushes it away from him, towards the shore, before slithering up after it. Others are edging on to the lake, but he shouts at them to stay away. Flat on the ice, he crawls towards us, pushing the bundle ahead, until at last she's safe.

At last I can move.

'She's mine,' I say. 'She's mine. My granddaughter.'

I push my way through. Someone is feeling for a pulse in her neck.

'She's alive. We need to clear her airways.'

They lie her on her back and push on her stomach. Water trickles out of her mouth. They push until the trickle becomes a flood, and then she gasps and her eyes open. Brown eyes, like her mum.

'Here,' I say, 'give her my coat.'

But someone's got there before me, wrapping her up in a big quilted jacket, cradling her head in the fur-lined hood. She looks like some sort of bug, big eyes staring out from a puffed-up body. I kneel down, and they pass her to me and I hold her like a baby.

'It's all right now,' I say. 'It's all right.'

One of her little hands is sticking out. I go to tuck it in and feel something smooth and cold, colder than her skin. Ice, I think, and I look down, ready to pick it out and throw it away.

Not ice. Metal. A chain spilling between her fingers. I open her fist. There's a silver heart nestled in her palm.

'What the—? Where've you had this from?' I mutter.

Her face is blank, eyes open but unseeing. The face of a doll.

I pick the locket up and drop it in my pocket, tuck her hand into the coat and hug her closer.

I look out across the ice. 'You're there, aren't you?' I murmur. Then, 'Thank you. Thank you for giving her back to me. Thank you for not keeping her.'

But did he give her back, or was she torn away from him by the brave young man?

I rock her gently. *Oh Nicola, you're safe now,* I think, *but you can't ever come here again. And you can't stay in this town. Not now.*

ONE

NICOLA, JUNE 2030

Something enters the pool to my right. It pierces the surface. Half a human – the top half, sliced through at the waist. Bright orange. It sinks silently towards the bottom, and as it turns in the water I see its face: bland, smoothed-out features. I can't take my eyes off it as it comes to rest on the bottom of the pool. There's something about the face, the lack of a mouth. It can't breathe. It can never shout for help.

A girl drowned at the weekend, in a reservoir just outside the city. It's been all over the news. I can't help linking the two in my mind. Two lifeless bodies under the water.

I've slowed right down, but now I increase my kick

rate. I want to get away from him. It, I tell myself. Just a plastic dummy, that's all. Even so, I plough forward, turning my head to the left when I need to breathe.

I hit the end of the pool seconds after everyone else. We bob at the shallow end, breathing hard. Clive, the team coach, walks down the line towards me. His whistle's in his mouth. His clipboard is clutched to his chest.

'What's happening with you, Nic? You're all over the place.'

The whistle drops out from between his lips as he starts to talk. It dangles on its cord between us, a silver pendulum.

'I don't know. I don't feel right.'

I don't want to be in the water with that thing lying at the bottom. The thing that was never alive. Drowning. I push up on the side of the pool and twist round to sit on the edge.

'You're better than this. You can *do* better.'

'I know. I'm not . . . I dunno . . . I can't . . .'

'Are you ill?'

He's giving me an out.

'Yeah, my stomach . . . I just . . .'

'Do you want to leave the session?'

I've never seen anyone just walk out. I don't know how serious this is. If I walk out, will they let me back next time?

'Yeah, I don't think I can swim like this,' I mumble.

He rests his hand on my back. 'It's nearly time anyway. Go and get changed. I'll see you tomorrow.'

Relieved, I get to my feet. As I do so, I look across the

pool. The lifeguards are clustered on benches. Training's almost over. Harry, tall and lean and blond, is preparing to dive in and rescue the dummy. He teeters on the edge, looking into the water at the rippling orange shape below. His skin is almost golden, kissed by the sun, his abs perfectly sculpted. His hands are by his sides, a moment of calm before he launches in. He looks up, checking that he's got an audience, looking along the bobbing line of seal-headed swimmers, and our eyes meet. He raises his eyebrows – a silent question: *What's wrong?*

Despite the heat I've got goosebumps up and down my body now, aware that he can see me – all of me, my shape, my curves – in this swimsuit. I like him looking and I hate it too. My self-consciousness hunches my shoulders and buckles my knees. I look away from him and start to scuttle across the tiled floor towards the changing room like a soggy hobbit.

When I glance back, he's leaning forward, arms behind him now, knees bent, ready to spring. He's poised, waiting for something. Then he sees me looking and he dives – arcing into the water in a perfect, beautiful movement, half-athlete, half-dancer. And in that moment, I know that what he was waiting for . . . was me.

His colours move through the water. He's almost at his orange target. It's too blurry to see the details, but in my mind's eye I see him reaching forward, wrestling the blank, mute doll into the right position to be hauled back to the surface. But the doll can never be saved. It never had life and never will. Why wasn't someone there to rescue the girl in the reservoir?

I've got the changing room to myself as I shower. The water pressure's pathetically low. It takes ages to get the shampoo out of my hair. Sometimes I wonder if I should cut it short – it would make washing and drying it so much easier. But I know I won't. Long, black and straight, a waterfall of hair, it falls halfway down my back. It's part of who I am.

The other girls pile into the room when I've nearly finished putting on my school uniform.

'What happened to you?' Nirmala asks.

I don't want to tell anyone about the way my mind flipped back there. I wish I could forget it ever happened.

'Stomach ache. You know . . .'

She nods, grabs her stuff and heads for the shower. We each follow our own rituals in here, the routines that make this kind of life bearable. I've worked my way through mine like I always do: deodorant, pants, bra, school shirt, skirt, short white socks, shoes, tie and watch. I'm warm from swimming, and I know that even though it's still early it will already be heating up outside. I'll leave my blazer until the last minute.

I squeeze the water out of my costume into the drain on the floor and wrap it up in my towel together with my swimming cap, then I move over to the sinks. There's a bit more banter now, a bubbling soundtrack to the business of mascara and moisturiser, hairdryers and lipgloss. Christie's preening, messing about with her hair, taking up too much space. Shannon and Nirmala step in front of her in a pincer movement, blocking her view.

'Hey! I was here first,' Christie protests.

'Yeah, and you've had your turn,' Nirmala says.

'I need to look my best. I need to look *spectacular*.'

'Why?'

'You know who's on duty,' Christie says.

'Who?'

'Who do you think?'

'Hotlips Harry?'

'Shuttup, don't call him that!'

I glance across at her. She's blushing, like I did when Harry caught my eye. He was looking at me, not her, but I don't need to brag about it. It's our secret. It's better that way.

'In your dreams,' Nirmala says.

'He's into me, he really is,' Christie says, slicking on rose-pink lipgloss expertly, pouting for the mirror.

'He fancies anything with a pulse.'

As we spill out of the changing room, I check my watch. Seventeen minutes to get to school. Perfect.

In the corridor, I'm in front of the others. I almost bump into someone, look up and it's Harry.

'Whoa!' he says.

'Sorry.'

For a few seconds his hands are on my shoulders. Fending me off, or holding me just where he wants me? I start to step sideways and as I do, he leans a little closer. 'You okay?' he says.

'Yeah,' I manage.

'I was watching you today. I always keep a special eye out for you.'

His voice is so low I'm not sure what he's saying. I keep

my eyes down, but my mouth tightens into a little smile. I keep walking down the corridor and out of the front door, and it's only when I'm across the tarmac that the words finally sink in. The heat from the sun matches the burning in my cheeks.

I knew it! It's me, not Christie. I look back over my shoulder, but the reflections in the glass stop me seeing anything – anyone – inside. The other girls have fallen silent. Christie's staring at me with her eyebrows halfway up her forehead.

'Nearly bumped into him,' I stutter.

'Or he nearly bumped into you . . .' Nirmala says. She purses her lips and fans her face.

'No,' I say. 'Just an accident. I wasn't looking where I was going . . . oh, there's my dad. See ya later.'

Dad's beaten-up Fiesta is parked by the side of the road, like normal. The driver's door is painted a different colour from the rest of it. He always watches from the gallery, and then fetches the car while I'm changing, so he's ready outside like a getaway driver.

I sling my swimming bag on to the back seat and get in the front. My second breakfast is waiting for me: a banana and an energy bar on the dashboard, a strawberry milk-shake in the cup-holder. I reach for the milkshake as the girls walk past the car. I catch Christie's expression in the wing mirror. She looks like she's sucking on a lemon.

'What went wrong in there? You poorly, Princess?'

I certainly don't want him to know about my freak-out. I had to fight to get my parents to agree to my swimming lessons. They were compulsory at school in years five and six, but Mum and Dad wanted me to opt out, although they'd never tell me why. I didn't want to be different, so I stood up to them. In the end they gave in and, when I tried it, I found that I was a natural. It was like the water had been waiting for me all that time.

'It's nothing. Just got a bit of a stomach cramp. I'm fine.'

He's nudging out into the traffic as we talk. Somebody blasts their horn, loud and startling through our open windows. Dad raises his hand, half-thanks, half-apology.

'Thank you!' he says, then mutters under his breath, 'Idiot.'

'Da-ad.'

'Hot and bothered already,' he says to me. 'Them, not me.' He glances across at me. 'All right now, Princess?'

I'm too busy eating to do more than grunt. I check my watch again: fourteen minutes to go. The traffic's bad, but it always is. To be honest I could walk it, but Dad's always here for me and I kind of like it. He makes sure my kit is ready, he drops me off and picks me up. He keeps his own records of my times and celebrates every improvement. It means as much to him as it does to me. Sometimes I wonder what else he's got.

The local news is on the car radio.

'Police have issued a warning to young people not to swim in open water, following a spate of accidents over the past few weeks. The hot spell has seen five deaths from drowning in the Midlands in canals, rivers and lakes, the most recent being the tragic death of teenager Sammi Shah at Turley Reservoir at the weekend. Inspector Ravi

Patel said that the temptation to cool down in open water is irresistible for many, particularly youngsters, but there are often hidden dangers under the surface and it's easy to get into trouble.'

I reach up to the radio to switch stations, see if I can find some music – something, anything else – but Dad catches me by the wrist. 'Leave it,' he says.

'Da-ad, the news is so depressing . . .'

'It's important. Ssh . . .'

We sit in silence until the end of the item.

'. . . so the message is, stay away from open water.'

Dad presses the mute button on the radio. 'Nic, you have to be so careful around water.'

'I know, Dad. I always am.'

'Yes. Yes, of course you are. We should know that by now, shouldn't we, with you doing so well? Our little mermaid? But even so . . .'

We pull into the lay-by near the school gates at the same time as my phone pings. Incoming text.

'I'll see you later,' Dad says, and leans over and kisses my cheek. 'You coming straight home?'

'Yeah, Dad. Early tea and an eight o'clock tonight.' He knows anyway. He's got my schedule off by heart. 'See ya.'

I grab my school bag and my blazer. As I glance back, he's pressing the mute button again and the news is back on. He sees me looking and waves. I wave back, then check my phone. It's from Harry: *Lookin gud this morning.*

I smile, pocket the phone and join the tide of people streaming into school.

TWO

It's too hot to concentrate in school. Even the teachers have given up. In lesson after lesson, we watch a video or a film, some of them not even vaguely related to the subject. It's like the last week of term, except that we've still got three weeks to go. The windows are open everywhere, and we've all got bottles of water on our desks. We've been allowed to leave our blazers off, and now we can play Spot The Sweat Patch as shirts stick to damp skin.

People are too hot even to muck about. We sit with glazed expressions, staring at the screen at the front of the room. And all the time, I'm thinking about swimming, about that other world that I belong to now, about the words that I can call mine: 'senior squad', 'elite'. That's me now.

Dad worries about water, but to me, it's a safe, constant

place. A rectangular body of water in a rectangular building. The smell of chlorine, the taste of it in my mouth, on my skin. I'd rather be there than anywhere else in the world. I'd rather be there right now, except that I can't quite get the image of the orange torso out of my head. The drowning man . . . and the girl in the reservoir.

At lunchtime I find my friends, sitting in a patch of shade in a corner of the field like usual. I settle down on the edge of the circle, not quite part of it. No one moves to let me in. We used to be mates, proper mates, but since I started swimming things are different. I can't go into town with them after school because I've got training. I don't want to drink or smoke or do anything that would affect my performance. Once you step back from people, you start to notice things about them, things you don't like. The way they talk about someone the minute they've left the group. Every time. There's always a comment, a smart remark, a little bitchy sideswipe. And now every time I walk away I wonder what they're saying about me.

I take the home-made sandwich, fruit and yoghurt that Dad's prepared for me out of my bag and sit listening to them. They're all talking about the girl who drowned in the reservoir. News travels fast and people are already filling in the gaps in the official story. Apparently she went to Stanley Green School, in the same year as us. Her sister plays clarinet in the Birmingham Schools' Orchestra. She was hanging out at the reservoir with her friends – they were all mucking about in the water when someone realised that they hadn't seen her for a minute or two. That's all it took. A minute. They reckon her feet got tangled in some reeds.

The chat goes on for a few minutes and it's almost like they're gossiping about any random girl — who she's friends with, who she fancies, who fancies her — and then someone says, 'What would it actually feel like?' And everyone grows quiet — all running a version of the girl's last moments in their heads. On your own. Water all around you. The rising panic. No one coming to help.

The lesson after lunch is unbearable. We're in a prefab hut with big windows down both sides. The sun beats into the classroom. Those in its glare are sweating and squirming in their seats. I'm on the shady side, but the air is still clammy and thick. It's English and we're reading war poetry. It's hard to think about winter and liquid mud and trench foot when it's thirty degrees outside. Mrs Goddard asks for comments on the lines we've just read. Her question hangs in the air like a week-old party balloon and floats slowly down to the floor, unanswered.

'Anybody?' she says. 'Come on, we can't go on like this. This isn't for my benefit. I've already got my A-levels. This is for you. You need to participate . . .'

We can't go on like this . . . it's been getting hotter for a couple of months now and I can't remember the last time it rained. It can't go on much longer, can it?

Selma puts her hand up.

'At last! Yes, Selma . . .'

'I feel faint, miss,' Selma says, just before she slithers out of her chair and into an ungainly heap on the floor. A couple of the girls near her scream. Others cluster around her, flapping their hands uselessly. Quite a few of them are fanning their own faces, like they're going to be next.

'Oh for goodness' sake,' Mrs Goddard bellows. 'Nicola, go and fetch Mrs Chambers.'

I willingly make for the door, happy to leave behind the growing panic. As I go down the steps, I hear another wave of screaming. I glance back and there's a second heap on the floor. They're going down like skittles.

It's too hot to run, but I jog down the path to the main school building and duck into Reception. 'We've got fainters in M4, miss,' I say.

Mrs Soubrayan rolls her eyes. 'Fainters plural?' she says.

'Two when I left, could be more by now.'

'I'll ring for help. Thanks, Nicola, go back to your classroom.'

The main building is Victorian, brick-built, solid and sprawling. It's cooler in here than either outside or in the classroom, so I take the long route back, dawdling through the corridors, cutting upstairs and along past the staffroom and the library. I stop at the water fountain and take a long drink. The first few mouthfuls are unpleasantly warm, but it gets cooler as it runs, drawn up from pipes deep below the school. I gulp it down, splash a little on my face. I pull my hanky out of my pocket and drench it with cold water, wiping it over my face and neck.

There's noise drifting in through the open window nearby. I go over and look down. Girls are spilling out of my classroom in twos and threes, arms around each other, crying. Staff are running towards them from all directions. What's happening?

I find the stairs at the far end of the corridor and head back to the classroom. The heat hits me again as soon as I step outside.

'What's going on?' I ask Tanya, the first girl I come across. She's sitting on the ground with another girl, knees drawn up, head leaning on her legs.

'It's too hot,' she says. 'It's too hot.'

'I know, but what's happened?'

'Everyone's fainting. Four, I think. Or five.'

'Oh, Jesus.'

I'm starting to feel light-headed myself. The possibility of keeling over is suddenly very real.

I'm just hot. That's all. I'm fine, I tell myself.

I'm still holding the wet hanky. I wipe my forehead again and the moisture brings some relief. I'm right by the classroom now.

'Are you okay?' a teacher asks as she draws level with me.

'Yeah. I'm fine,' I say.

We walk up the steps together. Inside, there's carnage. Girls are sitting and lying on the floor. A lot of them are crying, someone's been sick and the place reeks – it catches the back of my throat and I start gagging too. I clamp my hand to my mouth.

'If you're going to be like that, you might as well go home,' the teacher says to me. 'We don't need any more going down. It's nearly the end of the day anyway. Here, sign this paper and leave it by the desk near the door. Anyone going just needs to sign out.'

I don't need telling twice. I take the paper, find a pen in my bag, sign and print my name and leave paper and pen on the desk. Then I flee.

I thread my way through the classrooms and out of the school site through a side gate. I look at my watch. Nearly ten to three. School doesn't finish until ten past. I'm meant to go straight home. I've got time to walk home, eat and drink something and do my homework before Dad drives me to the pool for evening training. The walk takes about twenty-five minutes. Dad'll be expecting me at twenty-five to four. But I'll be there at quarter past, unless . . . unless what? It suddenly strikes me that I've got twenty minutes to myself. Twenty minutes of freedom. A tingle of excitement flutters up my spine. What can I do?

Like the robot I am, though, I feel my feet start to follow the programmed route, along by a second-hand car lot and a row of shops, then left at the food bank and past the boys' school. They come out later than us, but there's someone strolling out of the gates just ahead of me, tall and solid, briefcase in hand. He looks back and spots me. The sun glints on the thick lenses of his tortoiseshell-rimmed glasses. His face breaks into a broad grin.

'Hey, Nicola!'

Too late to turn around or pretend I haven't seen him.

'Hi, Milton.'

He's stopped to wait for me. Milton. He lives in my road, is in the year above me at school, but somehow I always think of him as younger than me. If I see him in the street, I usually wait a few minutes until he's gone. I mean, he's okay and everything, I don't hate him, but when we were kids he used to kind of hang around by my gate all the time. He always wanted to play, I couldn't shake him off.

'Study period last lesson,' he says, as if I'd asked him what was up, which I hadn't. 'I've finished my homework, so . . . how about you?'

'I got sent home. Everyone started fainting in my class.'

'Everyone?'

'Like, half a dozen of them, going down like ninepins. I was okay, so they said I could go.'

'What's wrong?'

'Just the heat and once one went down, they all started going. I felt it, too, like I could faint, but I got out in time.'

Talking about it now, the feeling sneaks back into my body. A hint of light-headedness, the rush of blood behind my eyes. It's just the heat, I tell myself, I'm not going to faint. Milton's feeling it too. Sweat is seeping out on his forehead and upper lip, his skin is glistening like black gold, but his tie is done up tight around his collar. The cuffs of his long-sleeved shirt are buttoned at his wrist, peeping out of the sleeves of his blazer. It makes me feel hot just to look at him.

'That's crazy.'

'It's scary. Looked like a train wreck or something, people lying all over the shop.' The blood starts to drain out of my face as I remember it. 'Everyone feeling worse, then feeling like the world's starting to spin, like you can't get your breath . . .'

Even though I've stopped walking, the pavement is still moving, rising and falling under the soles of my shoes. My legs start to buckle and I sit down heavily on the lip of a little wall with railings coming out of the top.

'Lean forward and put your head between your knees,

Nic. Honest, it'll help. Put your head down and breathe slowly.'

I do what he says. My heart's beating really fast. My breathing's quick and shallow. I've got to calm down.

I use one of the techniques I've learnt at swimming for controlling my breathing. I'm still hot but the panic's subsiding. The pavement isn't moving any more. I know I'm going to be all right.

In front of me Milton's rummaging in his bag. 'Here,' he says. 'It's cold. I got it from the water cooler just now.'

I raise my head. He's holding a bottle of water towards me. There's condensation beading on the outside of it. I twist the top off and take a swig. It's cold and flat and refreshing. I take several long gulps, feeling it work its way down inside me.

'Better?' he says.

I nod and hold it out to him.

'It's okay,' he says. 'It's for you.'

I take another swig, then screw the lid back on and roll the bottle up and down my forehead and then on the back of my neck. I wipe it on my shirt then try to give it back to him, but he shrugs.

'Keep it. Please. You need it.'

'Thanks.'

He grins and stretches his hand out to pull me upright. I hesitate for a moment. He notices and the grin starts to fade. He looks away and starts to withdraw his hand, and I reach up and curl my fingers round his. Our palms are cool and wet from holding the bottle. They kind of slide together and make a noise like a squelchy fart. We both laugh, then stop, embarrassed. He pulls me up and we quickly let go and wipe our hands on our clothes, mirroring each other: him on his trousers, me on my skirt. Clumsy, self-conscious. I don't want him to think I'm ungrateful, like I'm somehow wiping him away.

'Thanks,' I say. 'I mean it.'

''S'okay. You're welcome.'

I look at my watch. Five past three. My twenty minutes have nearly gone.

We walk along together. It's a while since we've done this. Years, maybe. I feel a bit ashamed for avoiding him. I mean, he's geeky and a bit awkward, but there's nothing nasty about him. He's actually all right, really.

'If you feel weird, just stop, okay?'

'I'm fine now. I always was, really, it's just . . . just . . .'

'Mass hysteria,' he says.

'What?'

'It sounds like mass hysteria, happens all over the place – schools, churches, factories. One person faints and then others follow suit. It mostly affects teenage girls . . .' He trails off, aware that I'm staring at him.

'Are you saying I was hysterical?'

'Um . . . that's one possible explanation, certainly.'

'I'm a hysterical teenage girl?'

'I wasn't labelling you. It's just something that happens. It doesn't mean anything . . . it just . . .'

'God, Milton. I thought you were being nice.'

'I was. I *am*.'

'No, no, you're not. You just think I'm a hysterical teenage girl.' My voice is rising higher, and I'm aware that

21

I'm sounding exactly like a hysterical teenage girl, but I'm in full swing now. 'You weren't there. You don't know what it was like. You don't know shit, Milton!'

I stop, aware that his body language has changed. His shoulders are hunched. His head is down. I've hurt him.

'I'm sorry,' I say. 'Let's just leave it, okay? Thank you for the water. I'm fine to walk on my own now.'

His head drops further.

'Okay,' he says. 'See you later.'

He stands still, in the middle of the pavement, and I start to walk away from him. It feels like I've just kicked a puppy and now I'm leaving it to bleed in the street, but I can't turn back now. I keep walking.

When I get to Mortimer Street, I glance behind me. Milton is walking twenty paces behind me. He sees me looking and looks down at the pavement again. God, things couldn't get any more awkward. I swing through my front gate and walk up the front path.

Dad opens the front door for me, like he always does, and Misty rushes out of the door in a blurry tangle of grey fur, craftily licking my knees and the back of my legs as she dances round me, her bushy collie tail swishing enthusiastically. Did Dad spot me out of the window, or has he actually been standing in the hallway? I've got a vision of him getting back in the morning, having dropped me at school, and taking up his post behind the front door. Standing there for seven hours. Just waiting.

'Hello, Princess. How've you got on today?'

I don't know where to start, so I don't answer and walk past him into the kitchen, Misty following close behind.

She follows me because I'm her favourite, and because I'm likely to slip her a treat or two when no one else is looking.

Dad's ancient laptop is on the table. There's a file onscreen – looks like a table or something. I only glance at it on my way to the sink to get a glass of water, and I don't really register the heading until I'm reaching into the cupboard and turning on the tap. Then the words form in my mind, like a headline.

Death by Drowning. That's what it says. What the hell?

Dad's followed me into the room. He casually closes the laptop lid, keeps his hand there for a little while.

'You haven't told me how your day was,' he says quickly, and even though I know he'll go overboard, I tell him about school and my walk home.

'Sit down, Nic. Sit down. You look pale.'

'You're only saying that because of what I just told you. I'm fine now.'

'They should close the school if it's too hot. If it's not safe.'

'Dad, I'm fine. The world can't just shut up shop because it's a hot summer.'

'I'm not saying that . . .'

'Yeah, you are . . .'

'I'm not. I just . . . I just want you to be safe.'

'Dad, you've got to stop this. I'm as safe as anyone else is. Life isn't a hundred per cent risk free. I can't sit at home for ever, wrapped in a duvet . . .' I stop, suddenly aware of what I'm saying – remembering the weeks on end, before I got on the swimming team, when Dad did exactly that, ground down by another redundancy, another rejection, another bill to pay. 'I'm sorry. I'm sorry, Dad.'

He won't look me in the eye now. He's examining his hands like there's something interesting in the palm. 'It's okay. I'll stop fussing. It's just . . . it's just that I care so much.'

'I know.'

He looks so forlorn. I put my glass down and walk across to hug him.

'I love you, Dad.'

'I love you, too, Princess.'

It's too hot to hug, but we stay like that for a while anyway, neither wanting to be the first to let go.

'Can anyone join in?'

Mum's in the doorway. She's got a T-shirt and shorts on, the ones she sleeps in. Must have just woken up – it's only an hour or so until her shift at the hospital starts.

'Gosh, Nic, you look pale. Everything all right? Something happened?' This time I get the full medical once-over – pulse, temperature, feeling the glands under my ears. 'Have you been drinking enough?'

'Yes.'

'Have another glass of water. It's so easy to dehydrate.'

'I know. I know, okay?'

'Sit down for a while. Or lie down. You mustn't overdo things. Skip training tonight.'

'I can't. They're picking the team soon.'

'Just one session.'

My phone pings in my pocket and I know, just know, it's from Harry. I hope I'm not blushing but I can feel an extra glow in my face. Whatever Mum says, I'm not missing training today.

'It's too important.'

She sighs.

'Your health's important too, Nic. I don't want you turning up in A&E.'

'I know, but I'm fine. If I don't feel right in the pool, I'll stop.'

'Okay, but go and lie down on the sofa. I'll bring you something to eat and drink.'

I crash on to the sofa and flick the telly on. Misty tries to jump up and lie on top of me, but it's too hot and I shoo her away. She settles on the carpet next to me with a sigh, just within range so I can twiddle with her ear the way she likes. They're showing the tennis at Wimbledon. Above the sound of balls being hit and players grunting, I can hear Mum and Dad talking.

'Sarita, did you see the girl, the one who drowned? Was she brought into St Margaret's?' Dad says.

'What girl?'

'Sammi Shah. She drowned at Turley Res.'

'I don't know anything about it.'

'Okay.'

Silence. Then, 'Clarke, it's been seventeen years now. You've got to let it go.'

'I can't.'

'It's not good for you.'

'I can't help it. I don't know if I ever will.'

The room is swamped with sticky heat, but suddenly I'm shivering.

25

THREE

'It can't be about me shouting at you. It's got to come from inside. Talk to yourself in the water. Be your own coach.'

Clive is giving us a pep talk before the final race for this session. He paces up and down the row, barking out his message, his words echoing off the tiled walls.

'This is it. I want to see a great start from all of you. I want to see commitment.'

I turn round and inch towards the front of the block until my toes are curling over the edge. The heat outside, my dad's weird behaviour, the reservoir girl, even the knowledge that Harry is sitting watching me from his lifeguard's perch, all melt away. There is only this moment, the block beneath me, the water waiting, the air in between.

'On your marks . . . set . . .' He blows his whistle to start us off. It rattles in my ears as I dive forward and then it's gone in the familiar busy, bubbling rush as I cut through the surface and am taken in by the water.

This is the best part of a practice session for me. It's not meant to be about beating the other girls, or trying to – it's about pushing for a better time than before. Trying to smash my personal best. But having the others swimming alongside boosts the adrenaline and of course I want to reel them in, overtake, surge ahead. Of course I want to be in front.

Talk to yourself. Be your own coach.

You can do this. You can do this. My own voice in my head, urging me on.

Through the oval lenses of my goggles I can see a line of darker tiles stretching ahead of me, dark blue in a sea of turquoise, like a path on the bottom of the pool, distorted a little by the movement of the water.

Come on. Come on.

I come up to the surface and now my ears are assaulted by the sounds of the world above – the splashing, the shouts, the reverberations of a busy, buzzing building.

I take six fast strokes before I twist my head round to breathe. I'm trailing behind Christie. Her feet are kicking spray into my face. Now it is about someone else. I don't want this turbulence, her second-hand water. I want to get out of her wake. I want to take her.

You can do it.

My muscles tense as I try to increase my power. My arms are stiff, like paddles. My hands slap on to the surface of the water. I thrash my feet faster and faster.

Come on. Come on.

I turn my head to breathe again. She's pulling away from me. Either she's getting faster or I'm getting slower.

No! Don't let it happen!

I'm getting close to the turn now. One good breath, a couple more strokes and I tuck forward, using both arms to turn a somersault in the water, reaching back with my legs to find the end wall and push off.

I'm at the surface too quickly. To compensate, I increase my stroke rate. I can feel the tension in my arms and legs. I'm moving like a swimming machine, a robot, my muscles rigid and unyielding.

Do it! Do it!

I'm running out of breath too soon, having to tilt my head every third stroke, then every second. It feels like the air isn't going into my lungs. It's whistling in and out of my windpipe but having no effect, so I have to breathe faster.

There's clear water between me and Christie now. I'm furious.

You've let her get away! You're an idiot! A loser!

I'm so caught up with talking to myself, so angry at the way my body's responding, that the end of the pool comes as a surprise. My fingertips smash into the wall and I quickly brace against it to stop my head following. I gasp and take in water. It catches in the back of my throat and I'm coughing and spluttering like a fool as everyone else bobs quietly in the water, holding on to the edge or floating gently on their backs, getting their breath back, letting their hearts slow down, basking in the luxury of staying still.

My throat's raw and sore where the treacherous water has tried to invade my windpipe. I try to inhale again and cough it out. I hawk up some phlegm, turn away from everyone and spit into the water.

'What happened?'

I spin round. Clive is crouching down at the side of the pool, clutching his stopwatch and clipboard. I was in such a state at the end, I didn't even look at my time.

I prop my goggles up on the top of my head. 'I don't know. I was trying to talk to myself and it just made everything worse. I got frustrated that Christie was ahead, got angry. Everything went wrong. My stroke, my breathing. I dunno. I was just rubbish. I couldn't do it. I just couldn't do it.'

I smack the water with the flat of my hand, splashing Clive, making him jump back from the side.

'Hey!' he shouts, and I know I'm in trouble.

I can't deal with it. Nothing he can say is going to be harder on me than what I'm already thinking. I duck under the surface, wishing I was at the deep end so I could sink down to the bottom, stand there with a metre of water closing over my head. Instead I fold my legs in front of me and drift down so I'm sitting on the tiles. My anger is turning to self-pity now. Without my goggles, the chlorinated water stings my eyes, but at least it washes away the tears that are starting to come.

I hold my breath and look around me, up and down the line of bodies huddling by the end of the pool. Black swimsuits and pale limbs. Skin scraped clear of hair. My thighs are lean, the muscles of my calves swelling gently outwards. I used to be really skinny and I'm still slim, but I'm stronger now. I like myself better this way.

I grab hold of my goggles and swimming hat and wrench them off my head. I was so bad today. So bad. I'm a swimmer now, that's who I am. If I don't have this, if I can't do it any more, what have I got? What's left?

My hair's tied up in a plait. I tug at the elastic holding it all together and run my fingers through, unravelling, freeing it, until it floats around me like a mermaid's. I move my head one way and then the other, and my hair swirls around me. And everything starts to feel right again.

This is where I belong. Today sucked, but it was just one race. It was just training. It's not spoilt for ever. I just need to do better next time.

I push against the floor and come up to the surface.

Clive is there, waiting, furious.

'You're lucky it's the end of the session, or you'd be on a timeout right now.'

'I'm sorry. I just want to win.'

His face softens.

'It's okay. I know. And you will. Trust me, you will win, Nicola, but not like that.'

Up in the gallery Dad is gathering up his things. Even from this distance I can see the black storm clouds hanging over his head. It's going to be an uncomfortable ride home in the car.

I haul myself out of the water and start trailing towards

the changing room behind the other girls. Out of the corner of my eye, I see Harry climbing down from his perch. I don't turn to look at him, but I walk a little slower, all my attention on him as he walks along the side of the pool towards me. We meet at the corner.

'Hey,' he says.

I look up, pretending that I hadn't noticed him.

'Oh, hi.'

'Bit of a temper tantrum you had going on there.'

I pull a face, feel myself blushing.

'No,' he says, 'I like it. I like a bit of . . . passion.'

The way he says it, it sounds like the dirtiest word in the English language. I'm sure my face is scarlet now.

I don't know what to say.

'Okay. I've . . . um . . . got to go now.'

He laughs and pretends to block my way, then stands aside. I walk past him, cursing my gaucheness. Why didn't I say something smart back? I could've just said, 'I bet you do,' and he would've thought I was sexy, sassy, instead of a bumbling, stupid kid. God.

My costume is hitched up round my bum. Do I leave it like that as I walk away? I can't. I pull the wet material down and as the elastic edge snaps back into place I hear Harry whistle appreciatively. I bet he thinks I did that deliberately. Well, I suppose it did make him look, didn't it?

'So what happened?'

Dad's gripping the gear stick so tight his knuckles are white.

'I dunno. I think I was trying too hard, and then when I started falling behind I just kind of panicked.'

'You were over one and a half seconds slower than your last practice race.'

'I know, okay? I know it was bad. It was just one race, okay? One bad race.'

I'm tired. I'm hungry. I don't need this right now. Seriously.

'You shouldn't have been swimming today. Mum and I were right.'

'Yeah, look, this isn't making it any better, you know? I just had a bad day, right? That's all it was. A bad day.' I wish I could stop the car right here and get out. I don't want to be stuck side by side with him, facing the third degree.

I fold the visor down on my side, but the evening sun is low in the sky now and the glare is still so strong that my eyes feel panicky in their sockets. The air outside doesn't seem to have cooled down at all yet. We've got both front windows down all the way, but the breeze wafting in is as hot as the air inside.

'I wish the air-con worked,' I say.

Dad sighs. 'We won't have the car at all soon. I'm putting it in the paper tomorrow.'

'Tomorrow?'

'No job, no car. Just can't afford it.'

The radio's on, as usual. Twenty-four-hour news.

'. . . a post-mortem examination carried out on the body of teenager Sammi Shah has confirmed that she drowned. Police today stated that there were no suspicious circumstances and they are treating the death as a tragic accident . . .'

Dad snorts and shakes his head. We're nearly home, just a couple of streets away. There are some kids playing on the pavement – not teenagers, maybe ten or twelve years old. As we drive towards them I can see they're having a water fight with some super-soakers. They're running in and out of the front gardens, crouching behind walls, bobbing up to blast a stream of water, and ducking down again. We draw level and one of them breaks for cover. He's smaller than the rest and his T-shirt is already drenched. He darts down the pavement, running alongside the car, screaming his head off. Two assailants appear from adjacent gardens and blast him in a twin-pronged attack. Silver plumes of water arc from the barrels of their blasters towards the kid. Towards us.

It's one of those moments when you can see what's coming, but it's still a shock. I scream as water hits the side of my face. It's cold, really cold. It ricochets off my skin, splashing the dashboard, the windscreen, my clothes.

Dad slams his foot on to the brake as the second blast hits him. It only catches the top of his shoulder, but instinctively he ducks down to see who's firing, and another volley hits him right next to his left eye.

Hot rubber squeals on hot tarmac. The front of the car has stopped, but the back's still moving, and for a moment there's that feeling that you get on a waltzer at the fairground, that sickening lurch as you're moving one way and the world's moving the other.

I'm holding on to the dashboard, squealing and

gasping. Dad's roaring like a wounded moose or something. The car comes to a standstill at a crazy angle in the road.

I stop screaming and let go of the dashboard. Dad's quiet, too, and for a moment I think that this is the end of it. We'll take a few deep breaths and then go on our way. But this isn't the end of it at all.

I look at Dad and there's a rage in his eyes that scares the hell out of me, a sort of cold fury that I've never seen before. He reaches for the door handle and yanks it open.

'No, Dad! No!'

He's out and round the front of the car in a flash. He doesn't go for the either of the guys that shot us – he grabs their victim. He gets hold of his T-shirt at the back of his neck, except it's not just T-shirt. You can tell from the kid's face that he's scrunching up flesh in his big, tight, angry fist, too.

'Dad, stop it!'

He lifts the boy off his feet with one hand. The other two are watching, open-mouthed. Their water blasters are down by their sides now.

'What the hell were you doing? This is a road, with cars on it! You shouldn't . . .'

He's shouting into the face of the victim. He turns him round so that the kid can see the road. His face looms above mine as I sit in the car. His features are distorted with pain and fear.

'Dad, he didn't even do anything!' I shout. 'Put him down, for God's sake.'

Dad ignores me. I open the car door and clamber out. I

34

reach up and put my hands under the boy's armpits, trying to take some of his weight.

Dad bellows at me, 'Get off him. I'm dealing with this!'

'No, Dad, you get off him. He didn't even shoot us. He hasn't done anything.'

Tears are starting to leak out of the corners of the boy's eyes. A new dark patch is growing at the front of his shorts and a trickle runs down his legs. He's wet himself.

'Dad, please, you're scaring me . . .'

'Put him down.'

I turn towards the voice.

It's one of the gunmen. He may only be twelve, but his voice is steady and powerful – he means business, and his water blaster isn't hanging limply at his side any more. It's pointing straight at Dad. In the next garden the other boy is raising his blaster too.

'Dad . . .'

Dad looks round now and sees what I see.

I so want Dad to put the little guy down and get in the car and leave. I realise I'm holding my breath.

He hitches his victim a little higher into the air, out of my grasp. The boy squeaks.

'You pathetic little tossers. Do you really think you can threaten me . . . with water pistols?'

The world stands still for half a second, and then . . . they let him have it with both barrels. They aim for his face, and as the water cannons into him he swears and lets go of the boy, who plummets to the ground and lands in a crumpled heap. Dad brings his hands up to his face to try and protect himself.

We pile into the car. The engine's still running, and we're off and out of range in a few seconds.

We're quiet until we get back to ours. Dad turns the engine off and we both just sit, in our soggy clothes on the soggy car seats, staring straight ahead.

'It was in my eyes,' he says. 'The water was in my eyes.' He scrubs at his face with the hem of his T-shirt.

'It's okay, Dad. It's only water. It's gone now.'

'The mess in here,' he says, eventually.

'It'll dry.'

He pulls the keys out of the ignition and holds them awkwardly in his hand, the edge of the key cutting into his palm.

'Dad,' I say, 'what just happened then? What's going on?'

'They shouldn't be messing with water like that. Don't they know there's a hosepipe ban?'

'I know. But they're just kids. They were just having fun.'

'Fun,' he says.

'Messing about with water. Didn't you ever do that when you were a kid?'

He turns to look at me. I think he's going to say something, but the words don't come. For the longest time, he just looks, and I feel like he's struggling with something, but I've no idea what it is and in the end it's too painful to watch.

'Let's go inside,' I say.

FOUR

The screen flares into life when I open the laptop. It's not shut down or locked or anything. There's nothing stopping me.

I know I'm alone in the house. This morning Dad got his ratty old jacket out and ironed a shirt. They're taking on people at a call centre in town – the interviews are this afternoon. He's worked on building sites and in care homes in the past, but he's applying for anything and everything now: call centres, cleaning jobs, whatever comes up. Mum's on day shifts this week. I won't see her until half-five at the earliest.

Even so, I check behind me. No one's there, of course. I turn back to the computer, and realise that my hands are shaking. I hesitate. Do I really want to do this?

I search his files. Right at the top of the list: *Death by*

Drowning. So I didn't misread it. I take a breath and open it up.

It's a table. Columns and rows. The column headings are straightforward – Name, Date, Place, Notes – it's the contents that are creepy. I scan down the page, trying to take it all in.

The ages and locations vary. A two-year-old toddler, found dead in a back garden pond. A nineteen-year-old lad who jumped off a weir. But they've all got one thing in common. They all drowned.

I study the table for a little longer, then I look at the next most recently used file. It's a map with a couple of dozen pins in it, highlighting locations. I fire up the internet, open my email, quickly attach the *Death by Drowning* document and the map to a message to myself, and send it. I'll look at them properly later.

I log out of my email, close the site and move the cursor to the end of the search bar. I let it hover over the downward-pointing arrow. If I click here I'll see Dad's most recent searches. I feel uncomfortable doing this, a bit scared of what I might find out. It's like looking at someone's diary – you just don't do it, do you?

I screw up my eyes so I'm seeing the screen through the protective blur of my eyelashes . . . and I click.

A dozen items come up in a list. Each one has an icon at the left-hand side, a title in black and a web address in green underneath. I scan down, ready to click again, to banish the list as quickly as it came if I spot anything disturbing. It's *all* disturbing, but there's nothing X-rated. It's just news sites – a long list of news sites.

My breath catches in my throat as I look closer. My stomach twists and for a minute I think I'm going to be sick. They are all the stories from Dad's table. News reports about people dying in water.

I click through them. I move the cursor to 'Bookmarks' and click again. Another list, but this is shorter. He's only bookmarked the stories about girls.

They seem to be in date order, the most recent first. The top link is a story about the girl in the reservoir. I know about her. On to the next one.

Authorities believe that they have discovered the body of 16-year-old Narinda Pau, missing for ten days. At about 6.30 p.m. on Saturday, investigators located a body at the bottom of a well near a field in Ledington, about 2 miles from the village of Oxlade where she lived with her parents and two brothers . . .

The body of a Watchet teenager was discovered on the beach at Minehead on Sunday and police are looking for clues as to what happened to her. Maddie Kaur, 16, was last seen on 17th May at the home where she lived with . . .

And on and on. Girls who drowned. Girls who look so alive in their photos. Girls who are all dead. So many faces. I don't think I'll ever be able to get them out of my head. But why are they in Dad's head? What's the connection with him?

For a long, sick moment the words 'serial killer' hover behind my eyes. He can't be. Not Dad. But that's probably what every serial killer's family thinks, isn't it? Otherwise they'd turn them in, or leave or something. No one could live with someone knowing they were like that, could they?

I think back to him losing it with the boy with the water pistol. I've never seen him like that before. He just snapped and it was like something took him over – his anger, I guess. He held that boy up for ages, just held him with one arm. Do I know him? Do I actually know Dad at all?

The palms of my hands are wet. My throat's dry and swallowing doesn't make a difference. I scan up and down the list of articles. Hang on, let's do this logically. A field in Gloucestershire, the beach at Minehead. None of these can have been anything to do with Dad. He was right here, wasn't he? At least he was here at eight forty-five in the morning and again at three-thirty in the afternoon. Could he drive somewhere in between, find a victim, deal with them and drive back by the time I got in from school? Could he disappear during the night? I don't think so.

And Sammi was with all her friends when she died.

So it can't be anything to do with Dad. But knowing that doesn't reassure me. There's something bothering him. Something to do with these girls.

I wish I hadn't started this. I wish I'd never looked.

I shut the internet and close the laptop. It's still only half past four. I've got time.

Misty pads after me into the hall. She makes to come up the stairs with me. 'No,' I tell her, 'get down. You know the rules.' She backtracks and sits on the hall floor, looking up at me reproachfully.

I tiptoe upstairs, feeling like an intruder in my own house, and push open the door to Mum and Dad's room.

I used to come in here all the time when I was little. I remember standing in the doorway and announcing to a dark room: 'I can't sleep.' 'I've got a tummy ache.' 'I had a nasty dream.' They never told me to go away. And their bed was a place of refuge – it smelled of washing powder, of the stuff Mum used on her hair to make it shiny, and of both of them. A good smell.

I walk over to the double bed and lean over to smell Mum's pillow. I know that this is a weird thing to do when you're sixteen, but still . . . and there it is. Honey and almonds. Mum.

I picture her head on the pillow, and Dad next to her, and suddenly I'm aware that this is where the stuff that happens between husbands and wives, men and women, goes on. Where they had sex. *Have* sex?

I straighten up. I want to get out of here – I feel dirty, inside my head and all over my body. My T-shirt's sticking to me. God, I'm gross. But I haven't even started. I need to do what I came for.

This shouldn't take long: it's a small room and there's not much in here. Either side of the bed, there are bedside cabinets, then there's a chest of drawers and a wardrobe. Each cabinet has a pile of books on it – his 'n' hers reading. They've both always loved books – they passed that on to me. The cabinet itself has a shallow drawer and a little cupboard underneath. But I can't bring myself to open a drawer. I've still got that three-letter word in my head, the word I want to wash away with soap and water.

I move over to the wardrobe and open the door. Mum and Dad's clothes hang like empty skins on metal hangers. Underneath the clothes there are shoe boxes, stacked up on top of each other. A shoe box would be a good place to store other things. I take them out, one by one, and lift off the lids. No surprises here, and nothing behind the boxes at the back of the wardrobe. I replace everything and move on to the chest of drawers. I work my way down methodically, riffling through, feeling right to the back of each drawer. I try to switch off, be mechanical, but it's difficult when the stuff you're touching is other people's.

At the back of Dad's T-shirt drawer, my fingers find something different. I draw it out – a roll of notes, kept tightly together with an elastic band. I pick it off and count the notes. A hundred and seventy pounds. Money scrimped and saved by a man who hasn't had regular work for years. I roll it up and fasten it again, and put it back where I found it.

There's nothing unusual in the other drawers: T-shirts and jumpers, jeans and leggings, belts and pyjamas and vests.

So, the bedside cabinets.

I'm looking for clues about Dad, so I guess I start with his. I slowly pull out the top drawer. There are hankies and coins and a box of earplugs and a packet of condoms. Oh God. I don't want to do this any more.

I start scrabbling through. Let's get this over with. The other drawers are no more use. Socks and pants crammed in, that's all. I push the drawers back in and walk round to

Mum's side of the bed.

My phone pings and I jump. The noise is too loud in the hush of this room. I check the screen: a new text message. I can't look right now. I switch it off and put it back in my pocket.

I pull the top drawer out until it's nearly at the end of its runner. Inside is neat and tidy. A collection of little boxes, some open, others with lids, make-up, earrings, and rings, ribbons and buttons. It's actually beautiful, like a miniature world, or a doll's house. I don't need to take things out. It's all one layer, neatly on display. I open any closed lids, allow myself to get a little lost admiring the contents, remembering the sparkle of a pendant against one of Mum's floaty tops, or the way a set of earrings catches the light.

I'm ready to move on to the little cupboard underneath when something catches my eye. Right at the back, there's something poking out above the side of a button box. I move the box a fraction and draw out an envelope.

It's an ordinary-looking kind of envelope; brown and small. There are three handwritten words on the front, and a date and some initials: Found with Nicola. 22/1/17. K.A. The writing is crude – hardly joined up, almost printing.

I turn it over. The flap has been opened and taped shut again. There's a lump inside, the paper bulging at the bottom. I run my fingers over it, then hold it between my palms, testing the weight of it. I hold the envelope up to the window, but the paper's too thick to let any light through, give me any clues.

22/1/17. I would have been nearly two and a half.

And this, whatever it is, was found with me. I was found somewhere. Where was I?

Something in my brain flips. If I was found, does that mean I'm adopted? Is this for real? A secret they've both kept from me?

My legs buckle underneath me. I sit on the floor as the room around me fades, blurs, falls away. All I can see is the envelope in my hands. It's the only thing in focus.

A little brown envelope.

Found with Nicola.

I can't stop now, can I? I mean, it can't get any worse.

I poke the end of my finger into the gap at one end of the flap, and work away at the tape, trying to tease it open in a way that I'll be able to stick back again. The envelope starts to tear and I give up trying to hide my handiwork. At the back of my mind I know that, one way or another, this isn't going back in the drawer.

I rip a little hole and peer inside. There's something metal inside. I hold my right hand flat, palm upwards, and tip the envelope. A round, smooth thing spills out: a pendant, followed by a chain. The pendant slips out of my hand, but the chain catches on my fingers, and then it's caught, suspended, swinging to and fro in a shaft of bright sunlight from the window.

And I get the weirdest feeling. The room's not here at all any more. The floor gives way. *And I'm falling, sinking, the breath shocked out of me by the cold. I drift down to a place sucked clean of colour and light. And someone says, 'Got you,' like this is a game, but it's not another little girl or boy. It's a deeper voice and I don't like it. I've hit the bottom now and I crumple and grab blindly and my hand finds some-*

44

thing, a cold, cold pebble. No, colder than a stone. And my fingers close round it and get tangled in its tail ...

Sweat trickles down my face and drips on to my hand. At the same time I hear the sound of a car pulling up outside. I scramble on to my feet, push Mum's drawer in, have a quick look round the room to check for any signs of intrusion and beat a hasty retreat. I've got the envelope in my left hand and the pendant still dangling from my right.

In my room, I stuff the envelope between my mattress and the wooden slats of the bed. Without really thinking I open the clasp of the necklace, reach behind me and put it on. I look in the mirror. My T-shirt has quite a high round neck. I pull it out in front a little and drop the pendant inside, then press the chain down towards my shoulders a little, tucking it away from view.

Found with Nicola. It's mine, right? So it's fine to wear it. It can be my secret.

Dad doesn't shout out a hello when he comes through the front door, the way he usually does. I hear the door opening and closing, the scrabble of the dog's claws on the tiles and Dad's footsteps going into the kitchen. I go downstairs to find him.

He's got his back to me. His jacket is on the back of a chair and he's tugging at his neck, wrenching the tie off.

'How did you get on?' I say.

He turns round and I don't need to see the shake of his head to know. His disappointment is written in his eyes.

'Sorry, Dad.'

'Two hundred and fifty of us for three jobs.'

'Sorry.'

'I'm starting to think I'll never work again.'

Standing there with his shirt sticking to his ribs, he looks defeated. The word 'adopted' doesn't mean anything any more, even if it's true. He's my dad, and I love him. I walk over to him and put my arms round his waist.

'You can be my manager when I'm rich and famous. You can carry my gold medals in a box when I do personal appearances.'

He gives me a little squeeze.

'Ha, that's right. We've got that, haven't we, Princess? We've got your swimming. Gonna get you to the Olympics, aren't we?'

I rest my head on his shoulder, and I think of all the times he's taken me to practice, the hours he's spent watching me. The last couple of swims have been dire, but I know I can do better. I've got to, haven't I? I've got to do it for Mum and Dad, especially Dad. What else has he got?

Underneath my T-shirt, the locket is pressed into my skin. It's uncomfortable, but I like it. My secret. Mine.

FIVE

As soon as I'm in the pool, my nerves take over. What if this session is as bad as last time? What if I'm just no good?

'Nicola, are you with us today?' Clive says.

'Yes.'

'I'm pushing you all today because the trials are next. Who swims in the regionals, who doesn't. Crunch time. You need to focus. Listen to yourself – your body, your mind. Only you can pull this all together. I'm getting worried about you, Nicola. Don't lose it now.'

Some of the others are looking at me, others deliberately looking away. I messed up last time, and now this. I almost feel like walking out again.

'Four hundred metres freestyle. Think about form. Think about your position in the water. Ready, girls? On to the blocks. Let's do it!'

Waiting for the whistle, I adjust my goggles. Harry isn't on duty today. I'm relieved and disappointed at the same time. I take a deep breath and then remember the necklace. I'm still wearing it, tucked inside my costume. I put my hand over the lump, and there's something comforting about it, knowing it's there.

As the whistle sounds I breathe in strongly. Then I tuck my head down, stretch out my arms and dive. I angle through the water, long and lean, using my legs as a tail fin. I start to head upwards.

Stay down.

A voice in my head, deep and loud, sending a disturbing spasm down my spine.

Keep under.

Obediently, I force myself to skim under the surface, flexing my stomach muscles to propel my whole body. My lungs feel the strain. By the time I break the surface, the need to breathe is intense. I turn my head, suck the air in greedily and press on.

Reach further. Reach.

It's not my voice, not the one I was trying to use to coach myself, and failing with. It's a man's voice, or a boy's. Illogically, I check both sides for the orange torso. It's not there. I try to put it out of my mind.

My arms are tense. I throw them forward in turn, scooping the water.

Relax and reach.

Relax. That feels all wrong. Swimming is about force and power, your body propelling water past and away.

Relax. I send the word to my shoulders and on through my elbows to my fingertips, and it feels like my arms are getting longer. There's more power there. It's easier. I'm not fighting the water any more.

Trust the water.

It's not a race, but, of course, it is. When I turn to breathe next time, I check my position. I'm not trailing at the back this time – I'm well up there with the others. I'm heading for the turn. I tumble forward, twist in the water and kick off again.

Stay under.

Again, I force myself to keep below the surface longer than I normally would. Once up, I breathe to the left. We're all pretty much level, with Christie, two lanes down from me, a couple of metres in front.

Relax. Trust the water.

This must be what Clive was talking about when he said, 'Talk to yourself in the water. Be your own coach.' I've found the coach inside me. I've found my voice. Maybe it had to sound different in order for me to take it seriously.

Trust the water. Trust me.

Everything's easier. I'm working hard, but it's taking less effort. My arms and legs are fluid. I'm enjoying this.

At the next turn, I'm almost level with Christie.

Reach further.

I power up and down the pool. I've found a rhythm now. Breathing every five strokes, checking alternately right and left. Part way through the sixth length I nudge in front and it brings a surge of adrenaline. I've got clear water ahead of me now. It's mine. The pool's mine.

Sixteen lengths in and I'm not tiring at all. I feel like I could swim like this for ever. I keep stretching, reaching, kicking until my fingers crunch into the wall. I surface and look across the pool, left and right. Christie's there too and I'm not sure if I've touched ahead of her or not. The others are a second or two behind.

Clive's looking at his stopwatch. I check up to Dad, sitting in the gallery. He's beaming, giving me a big thumbs-up.

Clive squats down and puts his hand on my shoulder. 'That's what I'm talking about!' he says.

I'm still breathing hard, my chest taking in deep lung-fuls of chlorine-rich air.

'So what was different?' he says.

'I listened. I listened to myself.'

'Yesss! I knew you could do it.'

He holds his hand up, inviting a high five. My hand meets his and I allow myself a smile, but it freezes on my face when I see the looks the other girls are sending me. I don't want them to spoil this. I don't want to give them that power. I duck under the surface and look along the length of the pool.

We did it.

Just for a moment, the maleness of the voice disturbs me again. I scan the turquoise space, looking for a flash of orange. The featureless face. The half-body. Is it him? Stupid as it seems, part of me thinks that it could be.

But there's nothing here. Apart from the line of swimmers strung along the deep end, there's only water. Of course the voice hasn't come from a plastic dummy. It was in my head, my subconscious, or whatever. The part of me that wants to be the best.

I bob up again. Clive's issuing the next set of drills. Backstroke now.

I hold on to the edge and bring my feet up close to my hands. I wait for the word, and, on command, I fling my arms over my head and propel myself backwards, arching down into the water, fishtailing with my legs and feet.

Stay down. Keep under.

The voice again.

Backstroke isn't my strongest event, but I'm starting to believe that I can do this. I can swim harder, longer, faster.

I can win.

SIX

'Were either of you going to tell me?'

We're all in the lounge. Mum's been to fetch Dad back from the police station where he was taken for questioning about the water pistol 'incident'. She got a call from him at work and raced home to pick up the car and then him.

'Well? Were either of you going to mention that you'd gone mental and attacked a boy in the street? Is there anything else you're not telling me? Has either of you robbed a bank recently or smashed up a shop?'

The boiling core that Mum has obviously been keeping zipped in for the last hour or so has erupted. Misty slinks out of the room, body low to the ground, tail between her legs. Dad and I look at the floor, at our hands, out of window – anywhere but at each other or Mum. I feel guilty, but I'm getting pretty angry too. I don't get why she's making this as much as my fault as Dad's. It's so unfair.

'I would've . . . it just didn't come up,' says Dad.

'Come up? You grabbed a little boy in the street! What were you thinking? What's going on with you, Clarke? You're thirty-two. When are you going to grow up?'

'They fired into our car. They fired at Nic. They got me right in the face. The water was in *my face* . . .'

'They were kids.'

'They got me right in my eyes. It was the water . . .'

'The water . . . God, Clarke, you've got to get a grip! This is getting silly now.'

'What about the water?' I say.

They both turn and look at me like they'd forgotten I was there.

'Nothing,' they snap, at exactly the same time.

'What?'

Silence this time.

'You never wanted me to learn to swim, you don't like water pistols, and Dad . . .' I stop, just in time. I'm not meant to know about the files on his computer. 'Dad's obsessed with the news, that girl that drowned. What is it? And don't say "nothing" cos I'm not stupid, okay? I mean seriously, what's going on?'

They look at each other for a long time.

Then Mum says, very slowly, 'Dad's got a thing about water. It's . . . it's irrational. Like . . . OCD or something.'

She nods at Dad, and he joins in. 'It's my problem. It's something I've got to deal with. I'll get help, I will. I'm sorry it's causing both of you problems too.'

Mum goes over to him and puts her arms round him.

'It's going to be all right,' she says. 'Come here.' She extends her left arm, inviting me into their hug. Drawn in, I let myself be hugged at first, then my resistance dissolves and I put my arms round both of their waists. I want everything to be okay. I want things to be how they've always been, to stay the same.

When we draw apart, Mum sighs.

'I'm tired and too hot,' she says. 'I'm going to have a cool shower, see if that helps.'

'What's going to happen?' I say. 'With the police?'

'I don't know. They didn't say, just took a statement and told him they'd get back to him. But we'll stick together. We'll help Dad through this. They might need to talk to you.'

'Yeah, 'course,' I say. 'But I don't want to — I mean, I don't know what I should tell them.'

Mum strokes my hair, like she did when I was little.

'It's fine. I'll be there. They can't interview you without a chaperone. Just tell them the truth. Telling the truth is always best.' She walks to the foot of the stairs, then turns round. 'There's nothing else I should know, is there?'

Dad hesitates.

'No,' he says. ''Course not.' He pulls a face and holds up three fingers. 'Scout's honour.'

Mum smiles and carries on up the stairs. But I'm not so easily reassured. It was the Scout's honour thing. Two words too many.

*

54

Back in my room, I open up my laptop. I don't believe this OCD story. Why hasn't it come up before? It just doesn't ring true. I find the email I sent to myself and open the attachment. *Death by Drowning.*

Let's start again, look at it with fresh eyes.

I read from the top, trying to take it all in, to see some patterns in the information. Name, Age, Date, Location, Death. I scan down each column. There's something about the ages. I thought they were all mixed up, but now I see that's only the boys. I highlight the girls' rows in turquoise, and it stands out, as clear as day: the figure in the age column is the same. All the girls are, *were*, sixteen.

Okay, that's something. I set up a second page, copy the table and delete all the boys' rows. Now I've got a list of thirteen girls, from all over the UK, who have died this year. I start doing what Dad must have done. Typing their names into Google, reading the articles about them. And suddenly, there it is – the names, the faces. They're all Asian, or mixed race. Just like me.

Thirteen girls.

And they've all drowned.

I click on Dad's map and look again. The map pins are labelled with dates. They're converging on this city. The drownings are getting closer.

I've got a heavy feeling in the pit of my stomach. This whole thing is sick – Dad collecting these stories about girls like me. Me looking at them.

I look away from the screen. This is crazy. These are all accidents, aren't they? Horrible, unfortunate, desperately sad accidents.

But Dad doesn't think so.

I don't understand. Maybe I don't want to.

I slam the lid shut.

SEVEN

It's quiet in the changing room. Everyone's focused on the business of getting ready for the trials. I'm trying to keep my nerves under control, but I'm buzzing with excitement. I'm pretty sure of my place in the freestyle relay team, but what I really want is the spot in the individual 400 metres freestyle. I was level with Christie last time. I need to go one better.

Christie's face is set hard. I can't see any sign of nerves as she tucks her hair into her swimming cap. I take my place next to her by the mirror. There's plenty of space, but she bumps my arm with her elbow as she turns to head to the pool.

'Sorry,' I say, like it was my fault for taking up too much space. I'm expecting her to say sorry too – for us both to smile, for everything to be normal – but she doesn't.

'I was off it the other day,' she says. 'Cursed with the curse, but I'm fine now. There's no way you'll come near me.'

She doesn't wait for a comeback, just walks purposefully out of the changing room, leaving me open-mouthed. The other girls heard her, but no one says anything. No one even meets my eye. God, what have I done? We're all here for the same thing, aren't we? To swim faster than last time. To try to be the best.

Everyone was so friendly when I first joined. I felt like I was one of the girls. I suppose it was just that I was younger than them, a bit slower, no threat. Well, I'm sorry, but I'm not going to slow down for anybody. Not Christie, or Nirmala or any of the others. If their fragile little egos don't like it, that's their problem.

One last look in the mirror. The locket makes a bump under my costume. Instinctively I put my hand up to it.

Found with Nicola.

A shiver runs down my spine. What do those three words actually mean? What's the story? I can't risk rocking the boat any more at home, but I wish there was someone I could ask.

'Nic, you coming?'

I look up. The changing room's empty apart from Nirmala, who's popped her head round the door to chase me up.

'Yeah. Yeah, thanks, Nirmala.'

I scurry across the grey tiles, past the showers, and into the little lobby that leads to the pool. Harry's the lifeguard today. He clocks me as I hurry in and I swear he winks at me.

'Okay, girls, warm up,' says Clive. 'We'll start the timed trials in twenty minutes.'

I slip into the pool. I've been given the lane next to Christie. She's already done one length and is swimming back towards me. This isn't a race, I tell myself. Not yet. All I've got to do is swim at my own pace, stretch my arms and legs, warm up my muscles.

I set off slowly, feeling the water with my first few strokes. I pass Christie midway along the pool. She's in her lane, I'm in mine. She doesn't acknowledge me, just powers along, expressionless. I can tell that she's in the zone, focused. But I'm all over the place. I'm thinking about her, about the other girls. About the police. About Dad. About Sammi, the girl who drowned . . .

Forget them. They're not important.

The voice is back.

This is what matters. Here. Now.

The voice is right. I need to let go. Let go of everything else.

Some of the tension melts away from between my shoulders. I reach up and over and forward. I pull the water underneath me, rolling a little as my other arm goes up and over and forward.

That's better.

I'm five or six metres from the end now, and suddenly I see a shape in the water beneath me. A knot forms in my stomach.

Another swimmer near the bottom of the pool?

Not swimming.

Lying there.

Pale.

Lifeless.

I turn my head and draw in a lungful of air. Then I jack-knife in the water and dive down. I can't see him now. I must have swum past. I twist around, but the floor of the pool is clear. Above me I can see the other girls, ploughing their straight furrows at the surface. Down here, it's just me.

The boy – and I'm sure it was a boy – has gone.

I float slowly back up and hold on to the side of the pool. I look all around, expecting to see a boy sitting at the side, or maybe padding towards the changing rooms. But he's not there either. Dad's up in the viewing gallery. Clive is at the shallow end, holding his clipboard, watching me. Harry is perched on the lifeguard's post. He's watching me, too. It's his job to watch, isn't it? So he must have seen him – the boy.

I haul myself on to the side and get to my feet. I can feel Dad's and Clive's and Harry's eyes on me as I walk round the pool.

'Harry? Did you see a boy just now?'

He leans down and his blond hair flops in front of his eyes. He flicks it back and holds it in place with one hand.

'What?'

'There was a boy in the pool. At the bottom. I thought he . . . I thought . . .'

He shakes his head and smiles.

'There aren't any other boys in here this morning, babe. You know that.'

'But I saw him. I—'

He clambers down the steps. So now he's standing next to me and Clive's walking towards us, too.

'Aren't I enough for you?' Harry whispers. 'You don't need any other boys.'

I'm getting flustered now.

Clive calls out, 'Everything all right?' as he draws near.

'Yeah, no. I thought I saw someone. A boy, lying on the bottom of the pool near the deep end.'

'A little boy? A baby?'

'No, a teenager. About my age, I guess. I'm not sure. I didn't get a good look. I—'

Clive peers towards the deep end.

'I didn't see anything. Did you, Harry?'

'Nah. There's no one here who shouldn't be.'

'But I was sure there was—'

I'm starting to wonder if I did see him now. What it was that I saw. If I saw anything at all. I'm standing here, trying to explain, and it sounds stupid.

'Nic, the other girls are well into their warm-up. You're putting yourself at a disadvantage right now. You'd better get back to it.'

'Yes. Yes, okay.'

My cheeks are on fire now. Everyone thinks I'm crazy. That I've made a fuss about nothing. Clive's stalking back to the shallow end. Harry puts his hand on my shoulder.

'You okay?' he says, and gives me a sympathetic smile, which just makes everything worse.

'Yeah,' I mutter, and walk back to my lane. I stand on the edge, looking down. The water is clear. No shadows lurking beneath me. No shapes that shouldn't be there. I dive in, grateful for the cool touch of the water on my skin.

And now I'm desperate for the rest of the world to disappear. I just want it to be me and the water. Nothing else. I want my mind to switch off and my body to take over.

Let go. Let go of it all.

Yes. Let it all go.

Trust the water. Trust me.

And I do. I trust the voice inside me. And I kick and pull and turn and breathe. The lengths seem effortless.

When Clive blows his whistle, I know it's time to race, and I'm ready.

We line up on the blocks. Beside me, Christie fiddles with the strap of her goggles. Perhaps she's nervous after all.

The whistle goes and I dive. I enter the water smoothly. I stay down for a couple of metres longer than usual and when I surface I hit my perfect rhythm straight away. I don't even check what the other girls are doing. I swim my own race. Lap after lap.

You can do this.

Only two lengths to go. And now when I take a breath I look to one side, swim five strokes and look to the other. There are two of us in contention, Christie and me. The others are way back. We're side by side. If you freeze-framed us right now, we'd be lying on the water, almost face to face, bodies flat.

It feels uncomfortable to be this close. Me and her. It's

personal. Like a fist-fight with no touching.

Just thinking this is enough to put me off. I've slowed down. She pulls slightly ahead.

No! Don't let her win!

She's into the turn before me. I roll forward in the water, twist my body and push with my feet. My head is level with her thighs. She's a metre ahead.

You can take her! You can do it!

The relaxed easy rhythm of the previous laps has gone. The adrenaline surging through me seems to be tautening the muscles in my arms and legs, but it's okay now. If the Zen feeling of being at one with the water got me through the first fourteen lengths, then maybe aggression will get me to the end.

Reach! Reach forward!

I try not to think about Christie, but she's right there.

Forget her! Reach for the wall! So close now!

I thrash my legs, driving myself forward. As each hand angles into the water, I stretch my arm out, straighten my fingers.

I hit the wall and look up at Clive. Beside me, Christie's doing the same. Neither of us knows who hit first. My chest is heaving. Even in the water, I can feel the heat in my arms and legs.

The agonising moment stretches out. Blood pounds in my ears like the ticking of a clock, filling my head, marking the time. It's like one of those reality shows when the lights go down and the presenter pauses before announcing who's going home. Just when I think I can't bear it any longer, Clive looks up from his stopwatch.

'Congratulations, Christie,' he says. It takes a split second for my brain to process his words, then the bottom drops out of my world.

I force myself to do what I know I've got to do next.

'Well done,' I say.

'Thanks,' Christie says. She's beaming. Too excited to be snide or nasty now. Just really happy. Feeling everything I would have felt if I'd been a split second faster. The other girls swim across, ducking under the lane markers, and soon she's the centre of attention. I stay in my lane, trying not to let my disappointment show. No tantrums this time. No tears. I try to cut myself off from my feelings, observe my body as it recovers from its exertion.

But the real me keeps coming to the surface.

It's not fair.

No, she won. I lost. That's all there is.

She cheated you.

She swam faster. End of.

You're better than that bitch.

She is a bitch. She is. I can't believe I let her beat me. I can't believe . . .

'There's no point sulking about it.'

I look round. Nirmala's leaning on the rope between us.

'I'm not,' I say. 'Honestly.'

But my face betrays me. That's what I'm doing and exactly what it looks like to Nirmala. Her eyebrows shoot up, wrinkling her forehead, which is trapped at the hair-line by her swimming cap.

'Honest, Nirmala.'

I bob under the rope and join the others, but none of them makes a space for me. I'm on the outside of the gaggle. It's lonelier here than in my own lane.

We carry on with more trials; I compete in the backstroke, but it's not my speciality. I come in third.

In the changing rooms, I try to shower and dress quickly, keen to get away from the others.

'So what was the fuss earlier? Water too cold for you? Sun in your eyes? Not happy sharing the pool with the rest of us?' Christie takes a deep swig from her water bottle. She's parked her belongings on the other side of the clothes hooks. She's got a towel wrapped round her and she's wiping her face and using another one to make a turban for her hair.

'No . . . I . . . I thought I saw something, someone, in the water, that's all.'

'Someone?' She's nearly drained her bottle now.

'A boy.'

God, why couldn't I just have made something up? This is humiliating. My face is burning again, but when I look at Christie hers is too. She's beetroot red and sweating.

'Are you okay, Christie? You look really hot.'

'I um . . . yeah, I'm not feeling too good. Just at the end of the session it felt like the water was heating up. Did anyone else notice that? Why would they crank the temperature up?' She drinks the final drops from her water bottle while the others murmur and shake their heads.

'I didn't notice anything . . .'

'I don't think so . . .'

'I was getting hotter and hotter,' Christie says. 'I guess it was just swimming so hard, my muscles producing the heat . . . and then the flippin' shower was boiling. I couldn't get it to run any colder.'

She notices her bottle's empty and goes to fill it from the sinks.

'That's not drinking water,' I say. 'Here, have some of mine.'

She turns back, takes a few wobbly steps and sits down heavily on the end of the bench.

'Thanks,' she says, taking the bottle from me. It's half full. She tips her head back and drains the lot. 'Sorry,' she says, handing the empty bottle back. 'I'm just really thirsty.'

'That's okay. Are you feeling better now?'

'Yes, I think so. Has anyone got any more water?' she says. She sits with her head between her knees for a minute or two, while the other girls fuss round her. Someone produces another bottle and she chugs that down.

After a while she tries to stand up, but she staggers to one side and lands heavily on the floor. Shannon screams.

'I'm okay. I'm okay. Who put the floor there?' Christie mumbles, smiling weakly.

I run round the row of pegs and help to lift her up from the floor and set her back on the bench.

'I think I'd better lie down,' she says, and slides off on to the floor again. She plants both palms and lowers herself on to the tiles, face down. 'Aah, nice and cool . . .'

'I'll fetch someone,' I say. I race out of the changing room to find a first-aider, Clive, anyone . . . I can see Harry lurking at the end of the corridor.

'Harry! Over here!'

He spots me, in my towel and nothing else. His face brightens and he starts sauntering towards me.

'Christie's ill,' I yell. 'She's really bad.'

The smile drops off his face and he breaks into a run.

'What is it?' he says as he gets nearer.

'I don't know. She's all hot and she fell over. She seems really confused.'

'Okay—'

He pushes past me into the changing room. 'First-aider coming through!' He crouches down by Christie. There's a folded-up towel under her head now. He puts his fingers on the side of her neck to feel for a pulse.

'Christie? Can you hear me?'

She turns her head a little.

'What are you doing here? This is the little girls' room . . . naughty, naughty . . .'

'Christie, have you taken anything?'

She wipes her mouth with the back of her hand. 'I'm thirsty . . .'

'She's already had nearly three bottles of water,' Nirmala says.

'I don't know what's going on. I'm going to call for an ambulance.'

It only takes a few minutes for the paramedics to reach us, two women in uniform with a couple of bags of kit and a stretcher. They blast into the room and cut through the crowd, immediately taking charge, asking questions, assessing the situation. We all stand back and watch.

By now Christie is hardly responsive at all. She can hear them, but her replies are nothing more than murmurs and grunts. Her eyes keep closing, and the paramedics battle to keep her awake while they take her pulse and blood pressure.

They quickly decide that she needs to be in hospital. She's lifted on to the stretcher and carried out of the changing room. It's all over so quickly. As the door closes behind them, a hush descends.

We finish getting changed in subdued silence. A couple of the girls are crying.

I put all my stuff into my bag. I'm on my way out when I notice my empty water bottle lying on the floor. The middle is crumpled where someone's trodden on it. The plastic has split. I pick it up and drop it into the bin.

EIGHT

Dad's right outside the changing room, pacing up and down.

'What happened?'

'Christie didn't feel very well.'

'I just saw her being carted off. What's wrong with her?'

'I don't know, Dad, she was just really hot . . .'

'Like heatstroke, or exhaustion or something?'

'I don't know. Maybe.'

'Are you okay? Are you feeling all right?'

'Yeah, I think so, just a bit shaken up.' But the truth is that now it's all over, I'm starting to feel a bit wobbly. 'I could do with a drink.'

He hands me his bottle.

'Here.'

I take off the lid and take a good long drink.

'Whoa, take it steady,' Dad says. 'Are you okay? Are you sure?'

'Yes, I just . . . I just want to go home.'

He ruffles my hair. 'Let's get you out of here. You can tell me about it in the car.'

Once we're on the road, the questions start.

'You got out of the pool at the beginning of the session.'

'That was just . . .' I've got a hunch I shouldn't tell him about the boy. Anyway there's nothing to tell, is there? There wasn't a boy after all. 'I just had a bit of cramp.'

'Cramp? In your leg? You weren't limping.'

'It had started to go off. Walking helped.'

'And you're okay now?'

'Yes.'

'It's the balance of salts, Nic. You must keep hydrated.'

'Ha! Like Christie? Didn't do her much good . . . you should have seen her, Dad. She drank three bottles of water in there, one after the other. I gave her mine. And however much she drank she just got hotter and hotter.'

'And the water didn't help. The water made it worse . . .'

It's like he's talking to himself. Thinking.

'Do you know how old she is, Nic? Is she the same age as you?'

'What's that got to do with anything?' And then I realise – his table, the girls. He's thinking about all those other girls. 'She's sixteen, Dad. Like me.'

'That place isn't safe,' he says. 'You can't go there any more.'

'What place?'

'The pool. You shouldn't be going to the pool.'

'Don't be silly, Dad, the pool's fine. I expect Christie just overdid it training. She's just exhausted or got heat-stroke or something.'

'I'm going to talk to your mother when we get in. If she agrees with me, that'll be it, you'll have to stop going.'

'Oh, come on. I'm not stopping swimming, okay? I love it, Dad. I'm good at it.'

'It's going to be difficult getting to all the sessions anyway soon, I think I've got a buyer for the car.'

'That was quick.'

'Yeah, should have upped the price, I reckon.'

'I can walk, anyway. I'll just have to set out a bit earlier, that's all.'

He sighs and shakes his head as he eases down through the gears to stop at the traffic lights. He puts the radio on while we wait.

'. . . this follows today's official announcement that limited water rationing will be introduced from midnight tonight. Non-essential users such as golf courses and car washes will be banned from using water. In some areas, a rota system is being introduced for domestic supply. The situation is under review, with the next step being the closure of public and commercial swimming pools, and the closure of some water-intensive industries that use mains supplies.'

'God, Dad, it's getting bad, isn't it? I'll have to stop swimming anyway if they close the pool.'

We take a different route home from normal, avoiding Wellington Avenue. There's something propped up against the front door. Half a dozen flowers, yellow and red daisy-type things, held together with a rubber band. They've been sitting in the sun and when I pick them up they flop down over my hand, wilted and sad.

'Hmm, nice flowers,' Dad says. 'Who are they from?'

There's a piece of paper tucked into the band. I pull it out and unfold it. The paper is off-white with a fine pale-blue grid printed on it. The writing is neat and careful.

Nicola, I hope you're feeling better.

It's signed, but I don't need to see the signature to know who the sender is: the graph paper has already given it away.

'Milton.'

'Two doors down?'

I nod. 'Don't ask.' I look to my left, half expecting him to be lurking in his front garden, ready for my reaction, but he's not there.

We go inside. Misty, flopped out in her basket in the kitchen, doesn't get up to fuss round our legs like usual. I put the flowers down, crouch next to the dog and gently twiddle her ears.

'What's up, Misty? Too hot for you?'

She raises her head and attempts a crafty lick of my wrist before resting her head down again.

It seems too harsh to just bin the flowers, so I start filling a glass vase with water to stick them in. The water running into the vase is cloudy and brown.

'Look at this,' I say to Dad. 'The water's a bit funny.'

I hold the half-full vase out towards him. It looks like it came out of a pond.

'What the—?'

As quick as a flash, he's grabbing the vase from me.

'Is this a wind-up?' he says, and there's a hard edge to his voice that I don't like.

'No,' I say, 'it's coming out of the tap like that.'

He lifts the vase up level with his face and peers at the water, turning it round, looking at all angles. It's pretty disgusting.

I pick up a drinking glass and hold it under the tap.

'It's okay, Dad, it's running clearer now.'

He snatches the glass out of my hand, too, and screams, 'Get away from the sink. Dry your hands. Do it! Do it now!'

His face is red and sweaty. His eyes are bulging in their sockets. The guy who went nuts over a water pistol is back, and he seems ten times scarier in a small space like this.

I back off and pick up a tea towel. He puts the vase and the glass down at the side of the sink and turns the tap off. Then he grabs another towel and starts to dry his hands. I watch in horror as he scrubs his skin so hard and so long that it starts to look raw.

Gently, I edge forward. I take his towel and tease it out of his grasp.

'It's okay, Dad. I think you're dry now. Shall I tip the water away?' I say, looking at the vase and the glass on the worktop.

'No,' he says, 'leave them. I want to show your mum.'

He's deadly serious.

'It's just water, Dad.'

'Look at all the stuff in it. All the stuff that came from our tap. In our kitchen. Here, in our house. I don't want you drinking this shit, okay? Bottled water from now on. Promise?'

'God, Dad, chill out. I'm sure there's a really simple explanation.'

He shakes his head. His breathing is very fast. The wet patches on his shirt have spread down both sides.

'Dad, are you okay?'

'Yes, yes. I'm okay. It's . . . it's . . .'

'What?'

'It's you I'm worried about. Keeping you safe. But you're not safe. Not at the pool. Not here, even.'

'But I'm fine. I'm absolutely fine. Look at me. There's nothing wrong.'

He won't look at me. Instead he's staring at the tap.

'Stay away from us,' he says, under his breath.

'What do you mean?'

He does look at me now, and it's like he's just woken up.

'Nicola,' he says. 'Come here . . .'

He opens his arms. He needs me, and right now I need him to be my dad again, to be normal. I want that more than anything.

I put my arms round his waist and he wraps me up in a sour-smelling bear hug.

'I love you, Nic,' he says.

'I know,' I say. 'I love you too.'

And I do. I love him, but he's scaring the hell out of me right now.

NINE

'Look at it.'

Dad's brandishing the glass in front of Mum's face. The water looks clear now, but a thin layer of brown silt has settled at the bottom of the glass.

'Was the water off during the day?' Mum says. Then she looks past him to the kitchen bench. 'Where did those flowers come from?'

'Um, they're from Milton,' I say. 'For me.'

'Ah, that's so sweet. What a gentleman. You should say thank you, Nic.'

'Do I have to?'

'Never mind the flowers.' Dad takes a teaspoon and stirs the water until it looks like the cloudy, brown stuff that came out of the tap earlier. 'Look at the water. Look! It came from our tap, in our house.'

Mum sighs and walks across the room. Her flip-flops scuff on the kitchen floor.

'Where are you going? We need to talk about this!'

'Nowhere,' she says. She rummages in her handbag, brings out her phone and calls a number. 'Denise? Hiya, love. Was the water off today at all? Ours has been running a bit brown. Yeah. Between twelve and two? Any warning? Hmm. No, that's okay. Yeah, fine, thanks. You?' She laughs. 'I know. Thanks, love. See you later. Bye.'

She ends the call and looks triumphantly at Dad.

'Off for a couple of hours at lunchtime,' she says. 'They sent a van round with a loudhailer half an hour before. That's all it is.'

He doesn't look convinced.

'It was the whole street, Clarke. Not just us. What's it like now?'

He's standing by the sink.

'I dunno,' he says.

'Well, have a look, then.'

'No, I don't want to touch it. I don't want you to either . . .'

He doesn't move.

'Clarke, don't be so stupid. I'm too hot and tired for this. Run the bloody tap or I will.'

She lurches towards the sink, but he blocks her. She moves to the side to get round him, but he grabs hold of her, pinning her arms to her sides. I've never seen them like this before and all of a sudden I don't want to be in the room, but maybe I need to stay, to protect Mum.

'For God's sake, let go, Clarke! Don't you *dare* put your

hands on me!' Her anger is white-hot.

He lets go and for a moment they stand there, half a metre apart, their faces mirroring each other in shock and dismay.

'I'm sorry,' Dad blurts out. 'I'm sorry, Sarita, I'd never . . . you know I'd never . . .'

'I know,' she says. 'I know you wouldn't. It's okay.'

She steps forward into his arms and they hold each other, rocking gently from side to side. Mum's kind of buried in him and Dad's resting his face against the top of her head. And now I do sneak out, but not before I've seen Dad's face: his eyes closed, his eyelashes wet with the tears that are leaking out.

I creep into the hall, but no further. I'm out of sight, leaning against the stairs.

'I'm sorry. I'm sorry,' he says. 'I'd never, never hurt you—'

'I know. It's okay.'

'It's not okay. You're my sunshine, Neisha. You make everything worthwhile. What's happening to me?'

Neisha? Oh God, he's said someone else's name. Another woman's name! This is going to go nuclear now.

'It's okay, *Clarke*.' She hasn't picked him up on it. She's stressing his name like she's reminding him what it is. What the hell? 'It's just too hot. Everyone's going crazy with it.'

'I'm not crazy. Something's happening. He's coming back.'

'He—? What do you mean?'

'All these stories on the news. There are too many of

them. Too many kids drowning.'

'Oh, Clarke, not this again. It's a hot summer. Kids seek out water to cool off in – they always have. You know that. *We* know that, don't we? And the more kids that are playing in water, the more likely it is that accidents will happen. That's all there is to it. Accidents happen, Clarke.'

'It's more than that, I'm sure of it. Look at the evidence. Girls the same age as Nic are dying. Mixed-race girls. I've found thirteen of them so far. And today one of her teammates fell ill at the pool. Christie. She drank *too much water*. The water made her *worse*. It could have been Nic. We've got to stop her going there.'

'Calm down. I can't understand what you're saying. What girls? What happened at the pool? Tell me slowly . . .'

'I can show you on my laptop. I've been gathering the evidence. Sit down, I've got it here.'

'Okay, but I'm really tired.'

'It won't take a minute.' I hear a chair scraping on the floor. Then it's quiet and I picture Mum scanning through the same pages I was looking at yesterday. Now and again Dad points things out and Mum murmurs in reply.

'Do you see? Do you see what I'm talking about?'

'Not really. Things happen all the time. Things go wrong. Why do you think this has got anything to do with us?'

'Look! All Asian or mixed-race girls. All sixteen. Getting closer and closer. It can't be a coincidence.'

'Of course it can.'

'It isn't. I'm sure it isn't, Neisha.'

'Look, stop calling me that, *Clarke*. What if she hears? So what do you think's going on, then? I know you're dying to tell me.'

'It's obvious. It's him.'

'It doesn't make any sense. Come on, Clarke, that was a long time ago. There's been nothing for seventeen years.'

'And now he's back.'

'Have you seen him?' Her voice is so low I can hardly hear.

'No. Have you?'

'Do you really think I wouldn't tell you?'

The laptop lid closes. The chair scrapes back.

'Let's stop this right now,' Mum says. 'You said you weren't crazy, but this . . . this is crazy. I don't believe it.'

'But the evidence . . .?'

'It's not evidence, is it? It's a bunch of sad stories that you've put together to fit your fear.'

'We should at least stop her swimming. Come on, back me up on this.'

'Stop her? You know what it means to her. It's her whole world at the moment. Besides, she's doing brilliantly. She could really get somewhere, Clarke.'

'But they're sixteen-year-old girls, Sarita. He's killing sixteen-year-old girls. It's too dangerous . . .'

'Nobody's killing girls. Girls are having accidents. *Boys* are having accidents. That's all there is to it. Anyway, think about it – the swimming pool is probably the safest place for her. There are always other people around. There are lifeguards watching the whole time. *You're* watching. God, Clarke, I'm too tired for this. I'm going for a lie down.'

The chair scrapes again. Damn, I'm about to get found

out. I open the front door and slip out as quietly as I can.

'Sarita, I'm really worried . . .'

'I know you are, but I can't deal with it at the moment. And we need to stop talking about it. Unless you want Nic to find out . . .'

I close the door behind me and stand with my back to it. Too late, Mum, I've already heard. But I'm not sure *what* I've heard. None of it made any sense.

It's him. He's back.

Who on earth was Dad talking about? And what happened seventeen years ago?

I don't know, but I'm sure as hell going to find out.

TEN

A noise to my right startles me. I look round and Milton is carrying a metal dustbin in through his gate. He plonks it down while he shuts the gate behind him, and then turns to look my way.

He sees me and looks away quickly, like he's been caught out. But he knows I've seen him, so he has to look back and now he presses his lips together in a sheepish sort of smile and half-raises his hand.

I'm the one who should be looking sheepish. After all, why on earth would I be leaning against my own front door? But his shyness tips the balance in my favour.

'Hey, Milton,' I shout, and start walking down my path.

He wipes his hands on his trousers and starts walking my way. We meet in the middle, on the pavement. It's still tacky from the midday heat.

'I wanted to say thanks. For the flowers,' I say.

He wipes his hands again.

'Oh, that's okay. I upset you and I didn't mean to.'

For some reason his straightforward kindness hits a chord. Without warning, tears start welling up in my eyes. I blink, quickly and hard, to try and get rid of them, but they're unstoppable. They spill out and flood down my face. I give a little gasp and then a sort of sob escapes.

Most people don't know what to do when someone else starts crying, and I'm thinking Milton's one of them. He looks at me and says, 'Whoa.' But then he digs in his pocket and produces a perfectly white, perfectly ironed cotton hanky. He shakes it out and puts it in my hand. Then he steps forward and puts his arms round me. He doesn't say a word, just holds me, and it's not pervy or awkward. It's solid comfort. Warm and quiet and human.

I don't even know what I'm crying about. The tears keep flowing until they stop. And it feels good, just to let it all out.

I use the hanky to sort my face out, and draw away from Milton.

'Better?' he says.

'Yeah . . . no . . . I dunno . . .'

We sit down on the garden wall behind us, perching side by side. The hanky is soggy in my hands.

'I'll, um, wash it,' I say. 'Thanks.'

'That's okay. You can keep it if you like.'

He doesn't ask what's wrong, and somehow that makes me want to tell him.

'Milton?'

'Yes.'

'Do you sometimes wish things would just stay the same and never change?'

'It depends on the things.'

'Home.'

'Oh. Nah, I wish things were different.'

'What things?'

'I wish Mum would be happier. I wish she'd be able to go out of the house sometimes. I wish she wouldn't cry so much.'

I haven't seen Milton's mum for years, but I've never thought anything of it.

'Is she . . . ill?'

'Agoraphobia. Depression. That kind of ill.'

He's so matter-of-fact about it, his face expressionless, staring forward, but when I slip my hand into his and give it a little squeeze, he squeezes back.

'I'm sorry. I didn't know.'

'Why should you?'

'Well, we live two doors down from each other.'

He shrugs.

'Behind closed doors . . .' he says. 'Anyway, what's changing for you?'

It's difficult to put it into words. I can't think of a label like 'depression' for the things going on in my life right now.

'I dunno. It's just . . . I'm not sure my parents are who I think they are. I don't know if I know them at all. I'm not sure they're even my parents. My dad's got this thing . . . this obsession, and they've both got some sort of secret.'

I like the feel of his hand. He's way bigger than me, but our hands kind of fit together. After the first exchange of squeezes, our hands have just sat together, no fussing. Now his thumb strokes the base of mine.

'Do you want me to help you?'

'How do you mean?'

'I'm pretty handy with the internet. I could try and find stuff out for you, about your parents.'

'Maybe.'

'And you could find your birth certificate. Then we'll know if they are your parents or not.'

'What would I look for?'

'Just an official-looking bit of paper. It lists your date and place of birth, your registered name, your parents' names.'

'Right, okay. I'll look.'

'And I'll do a bit of digging.'

'Okay. Thanks.'

I stand up and start walking slowly home.

'Nic,' he says, 'your mum and dad—'

'Yeah?'

'They've always seemed like good people to me. Don't be too hard on them. From what I've seen it's not easy being a grown-up.'

He picks up the bin and starts lugging it towards the house. Something about the curve of his back makes me want to hug him again, but the moment's gone.

'I don't feel like training. I mean, what if I get too hot like Christie . . .'

'I know, me neither. It just doesn't seem right, us being here while she's in hospital. It doesn't feel safe.'

I start to get all my things out of my bag. The others might have been put off, but I can't wait to get into the water. I feel sorry for Christie and I hope she gets better, but she's out of the game now. And I'm still in.

I put my stuff in a locker, make sure my hair's tucked in properly and my goggles are comfortable, and pad into the pool area. As soon as he sees me, Clive takes me aside.

'You know that Christie is unwell. Obviously, we have to make arrangements in case she's not back for the regionals. So, for the time being, you're our number one for the freestyle. That's what I want you to concentrate on in training. This is your chance, Nic. This is the big one. Are you up for it?'

'Yes. I really am.'

'Good girl.'

I know Harry's watching the whole time I'm talking with Clive. His eyes are still on me as I make my way to the middle lane and lower myself into the water.

'Fifteen minutes' warming up,' Clive says. 'Then we'll concentrate on technique.'

I push off gently, not kicking, just reaching forward, feeling the water around me, getting a sense of it. A pool is a pool is a pool, right? The same each time. Uniform. Except that it isn't. There are slight changes in water temperature, air temperature, the balance of chemicals. It's different every time and you have to experience it to understand it. You have to feel it on every inch of you, over and under, in front and behind.

I flip on to my back and do a couple of lazy back-strokes, then on to my front again and now I start to kick with my legs and scoop with my hands. Gently, stretching out, almost in slow motion. The water's beautiful today. I'm in ahead of the others. For a moment I've got the pool to myself. I ease my way down the lane effortlessly.

Looking good, Nicola. Swim to me.

I'm not even trying to swim fast, not competing at all, but the voice is there. I'm almost annoyed. It's broken into my blissful solitude. But the voice is me, isn't it? My subconscious coaching me. I'm still on my own, right?

I close my eyes, reluctant to scan the water, see what's there. But even with my eyes closed, I can sense a presence. I open my eyes.

There's someone there.

Underwater.

The boy is there.

I head towards him in the deep end. A pale, white body, drifting close to the bottom of the pool. I draw nearer and I can see his face. His eyes are closed, his mouth too. His short brown hair plays around his forehead.

It's the same boy. The one that no one else noticed. That not even Harry, on lookout from his perch, saw getting out of the pool. Who is he? Why's he messing about here when the pool is meant to be closed to everyone except the swimming club?

I won't get help this time. If he needs rescuing, I can do it. I'm as strong a swimmer as any of the lifeguards.

When I'm almost above him, I stop swimming and float at the surface, looking down. If I take a good breath,

I can easily dive down and fetch him up, but just as I'm about to raise my head to breathe, he opens his eyes.

I start to gasp, feel the water invading my mouth, catching at the back of my throat.

'Nicola,' he says. A stream of bubbles rises up from between his lips and heads towards me through the water.

His voice is the voice in my head.

'Don't be scared,' he says.

He's lying on his back, looking up at me. His eyes are pale, blue or grey. His gaze is intense. I don't want to look away, even though I need to breathe.

I can't believe this is happening. You can't talk under-water. Can you? How's he doing that? How is he breathing? How does he know who I am?

'I'm sorry I frightened you before. I didn't mean to.'

There are marks on his body, dark streaks, cuts and bruises. He's wearing white boxers instead of swimming shorts.

I can't look any longer, I've run out of air.

I jerk my head out of the water and take a quick breath. The murmur of voices bounces off the ceiling above me – the other girls are coming in.

I duck my head under again.

He's gone.

He can't have.

I dive down, swimming around in a circle, looking left and right.

Time to swim. Let's show those bitches who's the boss.

The voice is so close. He's right next to me, but I twist my head and I can't see him.

I'm with you. Don't worry. I'm here. Let's do this.

He's with me. He's the voice. Last time, I swam faster, better, stronger with him coaching me. Now, I'm freaked out.

I can't explain what just happened. I'm not sure I want to be here any more. He can't be real, can he? What happened can't have happened. But it did.

Another visit to the surface to breathe. I hold on to the lip of the end wall and look back down the pool. The other girls are swimming towards me, pushing a surge of disturbed water in front of them. The pool's no longer mine.

But it can be. Take it back from them. You can swim better than all of them.

His voice is seductive.

I'm still freaked out, but the tingle of fear is turning into a frisson of excitement. I want to believe him. I want to be better than the rest of them. I want to win.

I take an almighty breath and duck under the water. I push the soles of my feet hard against the wall, reach forward and dolphin my way through the water. My body is a wave. I'm part of the water.

That's it. Feel the water. Use the water. Be the water.

I stretch and reach and roll and breathe. I kick and pull and turn.

And no one can touch me.

ELEVEN

The improvement's phenomenal. I'm telling you, Mr Anson, it's not often you see something like this'

Clive's asked to see me and Dad after the training session. He's bought us both a cold drink out of the machine and we're sitting at one of the little round metal tables in the lobby.

'Whatever you're doing, keep doing it. Diet, rest, the whole lot. Keep this up for the regionals and we've got a rising star on our hands.'

Dad's trying to be serious, but I can tell he's almost bursting with pride. He's got his sensible, listening face on, but there's a little telltale twitch at the side of his mouth.

He gets his notebook out of his pocket, the one where he keeps all my stats.

'We haven't been doing anything special. I'm sure there's room for improvement. Diet, for instance. What should we be concentrating on?'

He makes notes as Clive talks. Protein, carbs, calories . . . I drift off as they discuss the technicalities. I know what's making the difference. It's not diet, or the schedule, or cross-training. It's the boy. His voice.

He told me I could do it, and I can.

I can't stop thinking about him.

His pale, thin body. The marks on it.

Whoever he is, whatever he is, wherever he's come from, he's good for me. He's my secret weapon.

I'm still a little bit scared. After all, I can't explain who he is or *what* he is, but I know I want to see him again, look into those eyes. Were they blue or grey? I need to get closer. I need to . . .

'Nic? That's right, isn't it?'

Dad's just asked me something, but I've got no idea what it was.

'Sorry, Dad, I was miles away. Tired.'

'It's okay, love. Time to get you home.'

We're walking, which is fine, except that today I could do with being on my own, having some space to think, but Dad's so full of times and training and regimes and schedules that I won't get a moment's peace.

It's nine o'clock in the evening, but the heat is still radiating up from the pavement. People are sitting outside pubs, music's blaring out of cars with their windows down. Ahead of us, two guys who are the worse for wear are having a drunken fight, aiming big swinging punches

91

at each other and mostly missing.

Dad puts his arm round me and ushers me over to the other side of the road. 'Tsk!' he tuts. 'You shouldn't have to see that sort of thing. Some people are animals.'

'It's okay, Dad.'

'I can't believe I had to let the car go.'

'It doesn't matter.'

'How are we going to get you to regional meets, national ones? We're going to need some more wheels, Nic.'

'If I'm really that good, Dad, we'll be able to get sponsorship.'

'Yeah, Clive was saying . . .'

'It'll work out, Dad, you'll see.'

He gives my shoulder another squeeze.

'Yeah,' he says, 'I really think it might. We could be on the up and up now.'

'So you're glad I came today? You understand why I want to keep swimming?'

'I do understand. Of course I do. I hate it every time you get in the pool, but I'm excited too. This could be something. You could change your life with this, change all our lives.'

'Hate, Dad? Why do you hate it?'

'It's just . . . I just don't . . .'

'What is it?'

'I'm not . . . I suppose I'm not much of a swimmer myself. It worries me.'

I've never seen Dad swimming. He never took me to the pool or the beach when I was little.

'Can you swim? Did you swim when you were at school?'

'Yeah. A bit.'

'Were you in the Scouts?'

'God, no. Why d'you ask?'

'You said "Scout's honour" the other day.'

'It's just a saying, isn't it? No, I wasn't in the Scouts. I wasn't that sort of boy at all.'

'What *were* you like?' He never talks about growing up, his family.

'I was just like I am now, only smaller. More hair. No tattoos.'

'What did you like doing?'

'I dunno. Just the usual stuff boys do. Mucking about, football . . .'

'. . . and swimming. So . . . there's no problem with me swimming, is there?'

He purses his lips and breathes out slowly, but he doesn't answer.

'I'm going to do us proud, Dad,' I say.

'Yes, Nic. I really think you are,' he says, but the doubt in his eyes is still there.

As we turn into our road, I can see Milton standing on the pavement halfway along. He's obviously waiting for me, but as we approach he pretends to be doing up the laces on one of his trainers.

'Milton,' I say.

He straightens up. 'Oh, hi,' he says, like it's a surprise to see me there. 'Hi, Mr Anson.'

93

'Hi Milton.'

Dad and I walk right up to our gate, with Milton trailing in our wake.

'I'll go in,' Dad says.

'It's okay, I'm coming. I'm tired. Been training,' I say to Milton.

'Right, it's just . . . er . . . have you got a minute?'

'I'm pretty pooped, actually. Will it wait?'

'Not really.'

Dad's standing near the front door, looking back at us.

'Everything all right?' he calls out.

'Yeah, everything's fine,' I answer.

Milton looks from me to him and back again. Dad goes in.

'So . . .?' I say.

'So, after what you were saying, I did a bit of research.'

'Okay . . .'

'You said that you didn't feel like you knew your parents. That you weren't even sure that they *were* your parents.'

'Right . . .'

'I asked you to look for your birth certificate, but all that stuff's online these days, so that's where I started.'

His glasses have slipped down his nose again. Sweat is trickling out from under them, running down the side of his nostrils, heading for the edge of his mouth. He pushes the glasses up and wipes his face with his white cotton hanky.

'Great! What did you find? Can I see?'

'That's just it. They're all online, except . . .'

'. . . except what?'

'. . . except yours. I couldn't find it.'

'What are you saying? Are you saying I don't exist, because, duh, here I am!' I hold my arms out wide.

'No, I'm saying that there's no record of you being born. Or rather, there's no record of Nicola Anson being born.'

'So . . . so my parents didn't register me.'

'Or they registered you under another name and changed it later. That's what I think must've happened.'

'Why do you think that?'

'Because when I couldn't find you, I started looking for your mum and dad, and I couldn't find entries for Clarke or Sarita Anson either. You, your mum and your dad don't feature on the official records at all.'

TWELVE

'So, who am I?'

Milton looks at me like he doesn't understand the question.

'You're the person you've always been,' he says.

'You know what I mean. Who are my real parents? Who are the people I'm living with?'

'I don't know. I'll help you find out, but I meant that other thing, Nicola. None of this changes who you are. You're the same person who woke up this morning. You're still you.'

'It doesn't change—? Of course it does! It changes everything! Everything at home is a lie! How can I live with that? How can I live with . . . them?' I can't even bring myself to say 'Mum and Dad' because those words don't mean what they used to.

'They're the same people. It's just . . . their names may have changed.'

It feels like the ground is falling away. There's nothing solid to stand on any more.

'I can't go in there now, Milton. How can I walk through that door?'

'Don't even think about it for now. Just breathe. It's going to be okay.'

I sit down on the garden wall and lean forward. Milton sits beside me. He rubs my back, and there's something about the feel of his hand on my spine. His touch calms me down. I take a few moments to breathe in and out, and I feel the warmth of his touch through my blouse, and the world starts to feel solid again. I sit up slowly.

'I need a drink,' I say. 'I've got some water in my bag.'

Milton gets the bottle out for me and I take a swig. It's not cool any more, but it's better than nothing. I chug some more and I hear the boy's voice. The boy from the pool. *They lied to you.* And it's true. My whole life is based on a lie.

'What a mess,' I say.

Milton pushes his glasses up the bridge of his nose. His other hand is still on my back.

'It seems like a mess now, but it'll be okay.'

'How can you possibly know that?'

'Your mum and dad are good people. That hasn't changed.'

'You mean the man and woman who've been calling themselves my mum and dad.'

'They are, though, aren't they? In every way that matters.'

97

I shake my head, in disbelief, in disgust.

'You know what my mum said to me, Milton? She said, "Telling the truth is always best." How could she? When she was living such a big fat lie?'

His hand is still there. Sweat from his palm has oozed into my blouse. I can feel it sticking to my back. I shift a little to try and move my skin away from him.

'It might not be a lie. It might be something else. There are all sorts of reasons for people to change their names. Sometimes they get help to do it, official help.'

'What? Like witness protection or something? Jesus—'

'Could be. I don't know. Have you ever actually asked them about your name?'

'No. Why would I? I didn't know anything was up until now.'

'So they haven't actually lied to you. Maybe they're protecting you, or themselves. We don't know the story behind all this.' He blinks as a little trickle of sweat makes its way from his forehead down the side of his face.

'Why are you defending them? I don't get it!'

'I'm not, I'm—'

'You can take your hand away now, Milton, okay?'

I stand up, shaking him off.

He holds both hands out, palms upwards in a gesture of defence.

'Nicola, I'm just trying to help. That's all.'

The wind goes out of my sails.

'I know,' I say, 'but this is really freaky. This whole day has been . . .'

'It's crazy. I get it, Nicola.'

'Milton, please call me Nic. You're the only person in the world who calls me Nicola.'

He blinks hard and I realise I've hurt him again. 'Okay, Nic. Okay.' He gets up from the wall. 'So what are you going to do now?'

'I guess I'll go in. It'll look weird if I don't.'

'You could come to mine.'

'Nah, it's late. I'll just go to bed.'

'Or you could look for your birth certificate. That might be the key.'

'Okay.'

I still don't like the idea of going home, but at least I've got a mission now.

THIRTEEN

Mum and Dad are both hovering outside the kitchen, but I can't deal with them right now. I go straight upstairs, close my bedroom door behind me and flop down on my bed.

I won't be able to look for my birth certificate until they're both out. God knows when that will next be. So maybe . . . maybe I just ask them for it, straight out. There must be all sorts of good reasons why I might need it. Passport? Driving licence?

I can't believe they've kept so many secrets from me. I don't even know who I am any more. It's all very well Milton saying that it doesn't change anything, but what does he know?

And what about my secret? The boy at the pool.

I'm almost too scared to think about him, but I can't

stop the sight of him appearing in my mind's eye. I can't help hearing his voice.

Trust the water. Trust me.

He's not real. He can't be. Just something I'm imagining. A really vivid daydream. I've always had a strong imagination. I had an imaginary friend for months when I was really little: Maudie, a girl exactly two months older than me, with long blonde hair tied in two plaits, and freckles across her nose and a laugh that sounded like she was crying. I'd make Mum set an extra place for her at teatime.

Maybe this is the same thing. I need a friend right now, and here he is. The boy of my dreams. But why has my mind covered him in cuts and bruises?

My phone pings. New message.

Hey Nic, wanna play? ;-)

It's Harry. Just his name makes my stomach give a little flip, like it always does when I see him or catch him looking at me.

I sit staring at the screen.

He likes me. He must do. Imagine if he was my actual boyfriend. Holding hands for the first time, first kiss, first . . .

I start to tap out my reply: *Okay. Lets meet up—*

Then I stop. Dad wouldn't be happy about me going out this late. But we don't need to meet, do we?

I delete the message and try again.

Can't get out right now.

Send.

I cradle the phone, waiting for his reply. It doesn't take

long for one to come back.

S ok. We can play here.

?

There's another pause, then, *ping*.

It's getting hot in here.

What does that mean? A minute later, *ping*.

Two words . . . and a photo.

A photo of Harry with his shirt off.

You next.

I can't help looking at the screen. He looks flippin' amazing and it's just for me.

For a moment another image comes into my head. Another topless boy – the boy in the pool.

The phone pinging again interrupts my daydream.

I've shown you mine . . .

Of course, he wants me to send a photo back. That's how it works.

I don't have to take everything off, right? I look down at my body. I'm wearing a T-shirt, which hasn't got much scope. I mean, it's either on or off. I fling the phone on to the bed and jump up. I flip the hangers along the rail in my wardrobe until I find a thin shirt. Just a few buttons undone – no harm in that, right? I'm just playing along.

I strip my T-shirt off, drop it on the floor, and look in the mirror. I haven't got much up top, but I'm wearing quite a nice bra today, which gives me a bit of shape. White with a pink ribbon threaded through the top. The necklace hangs down between my breasts.

I strike a couple of poses. Will Harry like me like this? Or this? There's nothing really bad about it, is there? I mean it's just like a bikini. So maybe I don't need the shirt . . .

I pick up my phone and take a few selfies, but they're too close up. You can't see enough. So I flip the screen and take a shot into the mirror. I check the picture. My face is disgusting. My body looks good, though. I delete it and try another. Yes, that's better. He'll like this one. He'll really like it.

I'm melting.

Attach object.

Send.

And wait. What's next, Harry?

My mouth's dry. I'm caught up in the game, but right now I'm not sure what game it is I'm playing, or where it's going to stop.

It's too hot to sleep. The windows are open but there isn't a breath of air. My top sheet is a screwed-up bundle on the floor. The sheet below me is damp where my body makes contact.

My head's full of pictures, words, feelings. It's like a tornado in there, churning restlessly, throwing out thoughts at random. Harry's bare skin. Dad holding that little lad up by the scruff of his neck as the damp patch on his shorts spread out. Mum: 'Tell the truth.' A screen full of names, dates, a map of locations. Drowned girls.

And a face, a voice. A boy who can breathe and talk underwater. A boy who knows my name.

Sweat trickles down the side of my face.

If I go to sleep who'll be in my dreams? Harry? The other boy? Or girls . . . desperate, panicking, drowning?

I sit up. I can't sleep, don't even want to.

So . . .

So maybe this is the moment to try and find the answer to some other questions. Time to look for my birth certificate. Mum and Dad are both asleep, or at least safely behind their closed bedroom door. I could look downstairs if I was really quiet.

I pad across the room and ease my door open. The house is dark, but I've known it for thirteen years. I don't need light to get myself along the landing and down the stairs. The step next to the bottom always creaks, so I step over that and I'm safely in the hall.

Misty pads out of the kitchen. I can hear her claws clicking on the parquet floor and see her dark shape looming towards me.

'Ssh!'

I grab her collar, feel my way into the lounge and close the door softly behind us, then I click the light on. It'll be fine like this as long as we don't make a noise. Misty, somehow sensing that we're on a secret mission and that I won't be able to shout at her, hops quietly – and illegally – on to the sofa and settles down. I wag my finger at her, but leave her be.

There's a small desk in the corner with shelves above. The desk has three drawers. I know the top one's got stationery in it – pens, envelopes, that sort of thing. Even so, I have a quick rummage through. There's nothing out of the ordinary.

The second drawer has a jumbled collection of takeaway menus, maps and tickets. I go through them carefully, but again there's nothing.

The third drawer is deeper. It's filled to the brim with documents of all sorts. I gather them all up and dump them on to the sofa between Misty and me. There are brown envelopes with all sorts of insurance papers, stuff about the car, tax forms. Some are labelled on the outside in Mum or Dad's handwriting. Others are blank. I go through them all, looking for clues. Some of the papers have Grandad's name on them: Anil Gupta. But I know about him, and I know Mum was a Gupta before she and Dad got married.

It doesn't take long to find the first piece in the puzzle.

There's an exam certificate, dated August 2015. A-levels. Three As and a B. And the name at the top: Neisha Manjula Gupta.

Neisha. The name Dad used when they were arguing in the kitchen. My mum's real name.

There's nothing similar for Dad. No GCSEs, no A-levels. No diplomas. And yet he's the real reader in the family. I bet you he's read every one of the books on the shelves in this room. He's the one who read me my bedtime story every night when I was little. He took me to the library every week. He's a bright guy, so what went wrong at school?

I carry on looking through, and then I notice Misty nibbling the corner of an envelope.

'No!' I hiss. 'Bad dog!'

I pinch her nose and extract the envelope from between her front teeth. There's a thick piece of paper inside. I draw it out and study it.

Certified Copy of an Entry Pursuant to the Births and Deaths
Registration Act 1953.
Date and place of birth: Twenty Second April 2014, Princess Anne
Wing, Royal United Hospital, Bath.
Name and surname: Nicola Manjula Adams
Sex: Female
Name and surname, Father: Carl Adams
Place of Birth: Kingsleigh, Somerset
Occupation: Labourer
Name and surname, Mother: Neisha Manjula Gupta
Place of Birth: Birmingham
Occupation: Student
And so on, down to:
Date of Registration: Third May 2014

So this is me. I'm Nicola Adams. And I think it means
that my parents are actually my parents. Neisha Gupta is
likely to be Anil's daughter, right? So she's my mum, the
mum I've always known. And is Clarke Anson really Carl
Adams? It's looking pretty likely.

Not adopted, then. That's a good thing, right?

It is a good thing – it's one element of uncertainty out
of the way – but there's another one in its place. What's
with all the name-changing? Why would anyone do that?

It's a little cooler down here. I put the papers back in
the drawer, but keep my birth certificate out. I sit staring
at it for a while. Misty has shifted round and is resting her
head on her paws. Her breathing is turning into a gentle
snore. I tuck my legs up, hitching them round the curve
of Misty's back, and rest my head on the arm of the sofa.

And that's where Mum and Dad find us in the morning.

Through cotton-wool clouds of sleep I hear their foot-steps on the stairs. I open my eyes. It takes me a minute to work out where I am. The light is still on above me, and there's a piece of paper on the floor next to me. Not just any piece of paper. I snatch it up and stuff it under my T-shirt, with the end tucked into the top of my knickers. I cross my arms and Misty hops off the sofa, as the door opens and Mum comes in. Neisha.

'Nic? She's in here, Clarke. What are you doing down here, and why's the dog here? What was she doing on the sofa?'

'I . . . I couldn't sleep. It was a bit cooler down here. I must have fallen asleep.'

'You'll be late for training if you're not careful.'

Training. Right.

I swing my legs on to the floor and, keeping my arms crossed, scuttle out of the room and up the stairs. I put the certificate in my school bag. I'll find Milton after school, chew it over with him.

FOURTEEN

*H*ave you seen this? It's all over the internet.

The message from Milton flashes up on my phone when I switch on as I'm coming out of school.

I click on the link and stare at the screen. It's a thread on some sort of forum. I try to take in the words.

The thread's been started by someone called kingsleighlad, who posts: *Too many deaths by drowning in 2030 to be accidental. There's evil out there. Evil in the water. Stay away from ponds, pools, tanks, lakes. Stay safe. Keep your daughters where you can see them. Don't let them be next. #evilinthewater*

There are thirty or more replies. Some arguing about the pleasures of wild swimming and linking to swimming sites, others picking up on the paranoid vibe:

Water's gonna get you.

only swim with friends in broad daylight

I never drink water, dude. Beer's much safer.

Kingsleighlad pops up again, responding to some of the comments and adding a link.

Don't believe me? Check this out.

I click on it and it's a chart listing names, dates, deaths. A chart called *Drowning Girls*.

Dad. It's got to be.

I go through the other links Milton's sent. They're all the same sort of thing. Warnings posted up in as many places as Dad could find.

I message Milton back.

Can I come over?

Yeah, course. Right now?

I'll call in at home first. Twenty mins.

I check in. Dad's in the kitchen, pouring his madness into the internet. He closes his laptop as he hears me approaching along the hall, and looks over his shoulder.

'All right, Princess?' The casual tone rings so false now, it's laughable. How can I be all right, with a dad who's hidden his identity from me for years, whose every waking minute is taken up with a weird obsession that he's now sharing with the world . . .

'Yeah, I'm just going out, Dad.'

'Out?' He looks at his watch.

'There's no training tonight, remember? I'm only popping down the road. To Milton's.'

'Look, if he's bothering you, I can have a word.'

'He isn't. I asked to go and see him. It's a homework thing. He did the same topic last year.'

'Oh. Okay. Have you got your phone?'

'It's two doors down, Dad, but, yes, I've got my phone.'

I'm halfway down the hall when he calls out, 'And don't drink the water there, okay? Have you got your bottle?'

'Got it!' I shout back and I'm out of the door before he can check anything else. Clean underwear? Hanky? Some emergency money?

It's still blisteringly hot outside.

I ring the doorbell at number 12. After a brief pause, Milton opens up and invites me in. The house is dark and stifling. I can hardly make out where to tread as my eyes try to adjust to the difference. All the curtains are drawn, cutting out most of the daylight, but there's a blue-white glow of a TV coming from the front room doorway.

'Mum's in there,' Milton says. 'Do you wanna say hello?'

'Sure.'

He leads me into the room. It's the same size as ours – all the houses are the same in this part of the road – but it seems much smaller. There's too much furniture squashed in, piles of newspapers and magazines on the floor. On a side table an electric fan turns one way and then the other. The place smells stale, like old kippers. The TV is an antique, a box rather than a flatscreen – must be at least thirty years old. It sits on a stand on the opposite side of the room. There's some sort of drama on: two guys hustling each other down a rubbish-strewn alleyway.

'Mum, Nicola's here. From two doors down.'

His mother is sitting with her back to the door. From where I'm standing I can't see her face. A hand lifts up and points the remote at the screen, freezing the action at the moment the victim is reeling back from the first punch, blood running from his nose. The hand waves the remote backwards and forwards, gesturing for us to come further into the room.

'Come in, come in,' a voice says. 'Let me have a look at you.'

I walk into the middle of the room and turn round. In the gloom, I'm not sure what's armchair and what's Mrs Adeyemi.

'Put the lamp on, Milton, I can't see nothing,' she says.

He switches on a standard lamp that sticks up from behind the back of a sofa, and now I see her, Milton's mum. When I was really little, she often used to visit. I remember her and Mum sitting at our kitchen table, cups of tea cradled in their hands. I haven't seen her for years. When did she stop coming round?

She was always a big woman, tall and sturdy like Milton, but in this room she seems enormous. She fills the whole of the chair. Her legs are planted firmly on the floor, furry slippers on her feet even in this heat. Her arms rest either side of her, obscuring the arms of the chair. There's a crocheted cushion behind her head.

'That's better. Is it really Nicola?' She looks me up and down. 'I don't think I've seen you since you were this high.' She holds her hand out level with her shoulder. 'Now look at you! All grown up!' Her face breaks into a wide grin, exposing a mouthful of bright, white teeth. I'm pretty sure they're not hers, at least not the ones she was born with. 'Ah, it's lovely to see you. How's your mum and dad?' she says.

'They're . . . okay,' I say. 'Mum's still working at the hospital. Dad's looking for work at the moment. How are you?'

'Mmph, you can see. I'm fine. I've got my TV and my Milton. He's such a good boy. He looks after me.'

Milton's shuffling his feet now. I'm pretty sure he wants to get out of here, but his mum's just getting into her stride.

'Ha, I can't get over what a beautiful young woman you are! You were always a pretty girl. My Milton, his eyes went like saucers the first time he saw you. You were moving in with your grandpa. What were you? Three? Four? My Milton had the hots for you, and I couldn't blame him! Sarita and I, we used to say you two would get married!'

She starts laughing and the chair quakes beneath her. She rocks backwards and forwards, slapping her thighs. The frame creaks under the strain. It's kind of infectious – I really want to laugh too, but when I sneak a peek at Milton, there's sweat beading on his forehead and he's grinding his toe into the carpet. He's mortified.

'So . . .' I say, 'shall we . . .?'

'Yeah. Yeah, we're just going to do some studying. Okay, Mum?'

The laughter's subsiding a bit, but she's not capable of speech yet. She nods and waves at us and before we're even out of the door, the telly's on again.

I follow Milton upstairs. The stifling darkness continues up here. I'm wondering if this is a mistake. He goes into his room and puts the light on.

'Excuse the . . . I wasn't, um, expecting company.'

I don't know what he's apologising for. Unlike the lounge, his room is pristine. His bed is made. There's nothing on the floor. His desk has no clutter at all, just his laptop and a desk tidy with some pens, pencils and a pair of scissors sticking out. There are posters on the walls, really cool vintage ones advertising 1960s and 70s sci-fi films. His bookshelves are things of beauty: books neatly shelved by colour, creating a rainbow along the rows.

He sees me looking and smiles sheepishly.

'I'm trying it out, the colour thing. Completely illogical, you know, can't find anything when you want it . . .'

'It's lovely. I'm going to do mine like that.'

His grin gets broader. I hate to kill the moment.

'Milton, those links you sent. The guy posting – it's my dad.'

'I know.'

'How?'

'They all come from your IP address. Didn't think it would be you or your mum.'

'He's been going on about this for months. He's obsessed.'

'What's he been saying?'

'He's just been focusing on news stories about drownings. He's paranoid about our drinking water – he lost it when the water from our taps ran brown. And he . . . he lost it again when someone shot at us with a water pistol. The police got involved. We're still waiting to see what's going to happen about that.'

'Okay . . .'

'I found that table he posted by accident. He'd left his laptop open and there it was. He doesn't know I know about that. He's been acting so weird . . . it feels like he's right on the edge.'

'That's what it reads like too.'

'Mum says he's got some sort of OCD, but that doesn't actually explain anything. I don't understand what's going on.'

It's such a relief to talk to someone about it. I end up telling him more. More than I thought I'd tell anyone.

'Did you look at all the links?' he says.

'Yeah.'

'Did you google any more?'

'No, I thought you'd sent me everything. Is there something else?'

He looks at me long and hard, but doesn't say anything.

'Milton, there's more, isn't there? What is it?'

He puffs out his cheeks, blows out a long breath and says, 'Come and look at this.'

He indicates for me to sit on the computer chair while he kneels on the floor next to me and calls up his bookmarks. 'Here,' he says. 'He's the one behind this.'

Onscreen is an online petition: *Close all pools now. Implement emergency water-saving measures.*

I read the full text. It's calling for a range of water bans to be brought in, but the main focus is closing public and private swimming pools.

'Why do you think my dad's behind this? The name of the sponsor is nothing like his.'

'Same IP address again. It's got to be your dad.'

'When was it posted?'

'Couple of days ago.'

'Shit, Milton, I don't understand. I really don't. He never wanted me to swim, but now all of a sudden he's my biggest supporter, at least to my face. He plots my training with Clive, he plans my diet . . .'

'. . . and yet he wants you to stop and he's doing everything he can to make it happen.'

'Why? Why would he do that? Why would he try to ban the thing that I love, the thing that could mean a future for the whole family?'

'He's scared, Nicola.'

'But why? This sort of thing – a phobia like this – doesn't come out of nowhere. There's got to be something, some reason why he's like this. I can't think of anything in the past year or so.'

'Maybe it's further back. A lot further. The rubber-ducky scene.'

'What?'

'I was reading a book on scriptwriting. It called it the rubber-ducky scene. When someone in a film or play remembers a traumatic moment in the past that made them the way they are.'

'This isn't a story, Milton. It's not a game.'

'I know. Sorry.'

'Why were you reading a book on scriptwriting anyway?'

'I was just . . . you know . . . it's something I'm working on.'

'What?'

'I'm writing a film. Sci-fi.'

'I thought you were into computers and stuff.'

'Yeah, that too.'

'Are you some sort of freakin' genius, Milton? Should I be getting your autograph now before you're too famous to talk to me?'

'Yeah, that'd be a good idea. Cos when I make it, there's no way I'll have time in my life for little people like you.'

He says this without a hint of a smile. He's so serious that I don't know whether to believe him or not, and then he cracks up. He's so dry, it's unreal.

'Well, I can't remember anything in my childhood that would make him feel like this. So maybe it was before I was born.'

'Do you remember where you lived before you moved?'

I think for a moment, trying to dig back. Suddenly I'm aware of the necklace inside my T-shirt. Even though I've worn it continuously for days against my hot skin, the metal is cold. Always cold. And, again, there's that feeling that I had when I found it in the envelope . . .

Falling, sinking, the breath shocked out of me by the cold. Drifting down to a place sucked clean of colour and light. And a voice in my ear. 'Got you.'

I should tell Milton. I should tell him about the necklace, but I can't, not yet.

'I don't remember – Mum and Dad never talk about it – but I've got this . . .'

I dig in my school bag and bring out the folded certificate.

'Brilliant, Watson!'

'No, not Watson, Adams. My real name's Nicola Adams. Look.'

I unfold it and smooth it out on Milton's desk.

'Neisha Gupta. Carl Adams. Nicola Adams. Kingsleigh. I can search for all those things. This is gold dust, Nic.'

'I think it means I'm not adopted, too.'

He lifts his hand to high-five me. I lift mine in response, but half-heartedly.

'What was that?' Milton says. 'That was like high-fiving a wet fish. This is a good thing — your mum and dad *are* your mum and dad.'

'I know. But who are they really? And why's my dad such a nutter?'

'I'm telling you, Nic, he's scared about something. If we find out what's wrong, it'll help. I swear it will. Shall we do it now?'

I look at the bottom of the computer screen. 17:35.

'I should get back.'

'Really?'

I shrug.

'I'm meant to be helping get tea today.'

'Well, I reckon I might pull an all-nighter looking at this stuff. No school tomorrow.'

'Message me if you find anything. I'll be at home, but I probably won't be able to sleep. Too hot. Too much to think about.'

'Okay.'

I pick the certificate up from the desk.

'Can I take a photo of that?' Milton asks.

'Sure.'

'Cool.' He snaps it with his phone, then hands it back to me.

'Thanks, Milton.'

'I'll show you out.'

'You don't need to – it's, like, down the stairs and out the door. I think I can manage that.'

'Okay, I'll just get started . . .'

He eases on to his computer chair and starts typing, his face lit up by the glow from the screen.

'Bye then,' I say. But his senses are locked in on the task in hand – he's lost to the outside world.

As I walk back home, a text comes through from Harry.

I want more.

Not now. I haven't sent him anything since the photo with my top off. I ignore him, but another message pings in.

What you wearing right now? Take it off.

I can't help smiling at the thought of peeling off my clothes in the street. And I can't help a little thrill of pleasure running up and down my spine at the thought of him sitting somewhere, looking at his phone, waiting. Waiting for me.

FIFTEEN

Hospitals freak a lot of people out, but to me the local General Hospital is just where my mum works. She's been a midwife for as long as I can remember. The antiseptic smell doesn't bother me, or the long, white corridors. But I'm nervous as I walk towards the Intensive Care Unit.

I feel like an imposter. We're not close, Christie and me. She doesn't even like me, but when some of the other girls said they were going to visit after school I felt that I'd be seen as a total ice bitch if I didn't come too.

'I'm not sure about this,' I say to Nirmala.

'It's okay. We'll just talk to her, that's all. We won't stay long.'

'Okay.'

There's so much stuff in Christie's room – monitors

and wires and tubes, flowers and cards – that at first it's difficult to see the person in the middle of it all. When my eyes do settle on her, she looks like a doll, a waxwork. Her mum's sitting next to her, holding her hand. She looks up when she hears us enter the room.

'Oh, hello girls,' she says. There are black circles under her eyes.

'Hello, Mrs Powell. Would you like a little break? A cup of tea or something? Nic and I will sit with Christie.'

'Well . . . I don't know.' She looks from us to Christie and back again.

'Have you been here all night?'

'Yes.'

'You need a rest, then. Something to eat and drink. There's a café near the entrance. Go on, Mrs Powell. Christie will be fine.'

'OK, then.' She stands up, leans over and kisses Christie's forehead. 'I won't be long, sweetheart,' she says. She gives us a weak little smile as she leaves the room. 'Come and fetch me if anything . . . if . . . you know . . .'

'Of course.'

I stand at the foot of the bed while Nirmala sits in the chair and takes Christie's hand, the one her mum was holding. 'Hey, Christie,' she says. 'It's me. Nirmala. And Nic's here, too.' She looks up at me and nods.

'Oh, um, hi Christie,' I say.

Then there's silence, apart from the electronic hum of the various machines in the room.

'I don't know what to say,' Nirmala hisses at me.

'Umm, just tell her what you've been up to, what's

happening at school . . .'

We're both whispering, and the absurdity of it and the awkwardness make me want to giggle. I can feel it forming inside me. Nothing about this is funny – poor Christie lying there, lost to the world – but that just makes it worse.

A snigger bursts out of my clenched mouth along with a spray of saliva.

Nirmala looks shocked, then suddenly she's giggling too. She flaps her hands in front of her face for a few seconds, then covers her mouth and turns away from me, but her body is shaking.

'Stop it!' Her words are high-pitched, almost squeaky.

'I can't!' My squeaks match hers.

I hold on to the metal bed frame, scared I'm going to pee myself. I cross my legs hard, and bend at the knees a little to try and stop the flow, but I just can't stop laughing. We're both helpless for a long minute or two.

Eventually the giggles die down. I've got tears in my eyes, and Nirmala's the same. We both dab at our faces with tissues and take some deep breaths.

'That was awful,' she hisses at me.

'Don't,' I say out loud. 'Don't whisper any more. That's what started it.'

'Right,' she says. 'Right. I'm okay now. Just don't look at me for a while, okay?'

'Okay.'

She starts to talk to Christie – about school, about the weather, about training. After the first few hesitant sentences, she's chatting away quite naturally – a one-sided gossip. I examine the cards and flowers clustered on her bedside cabinet. The cards are from Auntie this and Uncle that, the usual family and friends. I pick up one from near the front. It's got a picture of a teddy bear on the front, holding a red heart. Inside it says, *To the best girlfriend ever, Get Well Soon, with all my love, Harry xxxxxxxxx*

The best girlfriend ever?

I turn around. Nirmala's still chatting away.

' . . . really thinks he fancies her, but I heard he was doing it for a bet . . .'

'Nirmala—?'

'What?'

'This card . . .'

'What about it?'

'Have you seen it?'

'No. I don't know. Why?'

I hand it over. She looks at the front and reads the inside.

'Ah, that's sweet,' she says and hands it back to me.

'Is he—? I mean, are they—?'

She smiles.

'Yeah,' she says. 'It's meant to be a secret, but everyone knows. They've been going out for nearly a month now.'

I guess my jaw must have dropped, because she looks at me and frowns.

'What?'

I shut my mouth and try to get myself together.

'Nothing. I just . . . I just didn't know.'

'He's really into her, it's so sweet. He's been in pieces since she's been here.'

122

'Yeah. Right. Poor Harry.'

I want more. What are you wearing right now? Take it off.

I can feel myself going hot all over.

'Nic? You all right?'

'Yeah, just feel a bit . . .'

'Look, you sit down here for a minute. It's your turn anyway. Talk to Christie.'

I walk round to the other side of the bed and sit down.

The white sheet rises and falls gently as Christie breathes in and out. Her face is completely still, eyes closed, mouth slightly open. I think of her hot and sweaty and gasping for water in the changing rooms. I think of her hot and sweaty with Harry . . . but it's not just sex with them, is it? They're going out. They're 'sweet' together.

He loves her, not me.

I'm just a bit on the side. Someone to be used. A nobody.

My phone pings. I glance down. Harry: *Wot you doing now, sexy?*

Oh my God. I feel so dirty, used. I put my phone away.

'It was you all the time. Of course it was,' I say to her, under my breath.

Nirmala looks at me, frowning.

'What did you say?'

I ignore her and study Christie's face, trying to see what she has and I don't. What it is that makes her the sort of girl boys fall in love with, and me the sort they want to mess about.

And as I stare at her . . . there's a flicker, a hint of

movement at the corner of one of her eyes.

'Nirmala! Did you see that? Look! She's waking up!'

We huddle closer.

'I can't see anything. I can't . . . oh my God!'

Christie's eyelids flutter. Open, shut, open again.

'Christie!' Nirmala squeaks. 'Oh my God, Christie!'

She grabs her hand and squeezes it. Christie's eyes are darting left and right. She seems to have difficulty focusing. Then she sees me. Our eyes meet and I feel like a rabbit caught in the headlights.

'Oh my God, this is amazing!' Nirmala shouts. 'I'll go and fetch her mum!' She sprints out of the room, and we're alone together. Me and the girl I betrayed. But she doesn't know, does she? Nobody knows.

But still she stares at me, and I feel sweat pricking at my scalp.

Her sore, cracked lips move apart a little.

The tip of her tongue comes out, moves left and right over her lips.

The tendons in her neck stand out as she tries to strain her head forward.

I put my hand on her forehead, the way my mum used to do when I was ill.

'Steady, Christie. It's all right. Your mum will be here soon. The nurses . . .' I don't know if it's me or her I'm trying to reassure.

Her lips move together again. She purses them and makes a croaking noise. She's trying to speak.

I move my head closer, tip my ear near to her mouth.

'Waaw,' she whispers.

'What? What was that?'

She tries again.

'War . . . ter. . .'

She's thirsty. I remember her staggering around the changing room, slugging back bottle after bottle.

'I don't know if I should . . .'

There's a white plastic beaker on the cabinet next to the bed, and a jug with a lid, half-full of water.

'Maybe just a little . . .'

I pour some water into the cup. Then I slide one hand behind her head to support it and gently bring the lip of the cup to her mouth. She grunts, which I take as encouragement. I tip the cup and water trickles in. A little spills down her chin. The grunting turns to coughing. Tiny drops spray into my face. Her body jerks.

Appalled, I put the cup down and slide my hand further behind her, trying to rub the top of her back, soothe her somehow.

Her eyes are bulging in their sockets.

'What are you doing?' I turn round as a nurse bustles into the room.

Suddenly the room is full of people. Alarms are going off. I'm pushed out of the way and retreat into a corner, from where I watch a team of nurses cluster around her, shout at her, shout at each other.

Christie's mum stands in the doorway, Nirmala close behind. One of the nurses darts to the door and closes it in their faces. Then she spots me, grabs my arm and propels me towards the door. 'You can't stay here!'

And now I'm out of the room, the door is closed again

and I'm standing looking directly into Mrs Powell's shocked face.

'My baby,' she gasps. 'What are they doing to my baby?'

I turn round. Through the criss-crossed square of glass at eye level, I can see the nurses applying a couple of large, rectangular paddles with wires coming out of them to Christie's bare chest. I turn back, not wanting to see the jolt in her body as they deliver the electric shock.

'They're just . . . I'm sure it's going to be . . .'

'What happened?' she says to me. She clutches both of my arms. 'What happened just now?'

'She woke up. She asked me for some water.'

'She spoke to you?'

'Yes . . . sort of. Just one word. "Water." And she was trying to lick her lips.'

'And you gave it to her?'

'Um . . . yes.'

Her hands are gripping me so tightly now it hurts.

'That's what was killing her. Too much water. Swelling her brain. Killing her from the inside!'

The veins in her temples are standing out. Her fingers are digging in so hard, I swear she'll break my skin in a minute.

'I'm sorry. I didn't know . . . she's going to be okay. They're doing everything . . .'

The door behind me opens. A doctor stands in the doorway.

Behind her the room is quiet. Figures move around the bed silently, putting things away, covering Christie's naked chest up.

'Mrs Powell?' the doctor says.

She lets go of me and I step to one side. She searches the doctor's face and says, 'Don't say it. Don't tell me.'

'Mrs Powell, I'm so sorry. We did everything we could.'

'No. Don't tell me my baby's dead. No, no, no, no, no!' She looks wildly about her for a moment before fixing on me. 'You've killed her! You!' Angry tears spill down her face.

Nirmala and the doctor stare at me.

'I didn't mean . . . I'm sorry! I'm sorry!' I say as I twist away from them and start running down the corridor. This is all a mistake. I'll wake up in a minute, in my own bed, in my own room . . . and this will be gone, just a half-remembered nightmare.

I'll wake up. Won't I?

SIXTEEN

'Why didn't you answer my texts?'
'I didn't get them!'
'Nic, don't take me for a fool. You got them.'
'I didn't have my phone on, okay? I'd switched it off. I needed a bit of time on my own. Christie died, Dad. I was there, right? I *saw* her die. I needed . . . I just wanted to . . .'
'It's okay, we understand, don't we, Clarke?' Mum's placed herself between Dad and me in the hallway. She's holding my hand now.
'You can't just run off, Nic.' Dad's not giving up. 'Your mum and me have been worried out of our minds.'
'I was only gone a couple of hours. What's the big deal?'
'You just said it yourself. Christie's dead. Everything changes now.'

'I don't get it. What changes?'

'You're in danger, Nic. Real danger. You have to listen to me. You have to do what I say.'

'Clarke, please . . .' Mum holds her other hand up, as if that will stop him.

'Sarita, you've got to back me up. You can't ignore the evidence any more.'

'Not in front of Nic, Clarke, please. She's upset. We need to concentrate on her.'

'That's exactly what I am doing. Thinking of her.'

'For God's sake, you two, this isn't about me! It's not about you, either. It's about Christie. My friend. My friend's dead.'

Tears spill down my face and they're real, but I don't know if I'm crying for Christie or for me.

I gave her the water that killed her. However I play it in my head, wherever I go, the truth doesn't change. It comes with me. It won't ever go away.

I killed Christie. As good as. I'm going to have to live with that for the rest of my life.

'Of course,' Mum soothes. 'You've had a shock.' She puts her arms round me, hugs me close.

'I didn't mean for this to happen,' I blubber. 'Why can't everything just stay the same?'

'Ssh!' she says into my hair. 'It's all right. It's all right.'

But it isn't, is it? How can anything ever be all right again?

'I want to lie down.'

'Of course. You go up. Take a bit of time. Dad and I will be here if you need us.'

I start to walk up the stairs.

'Sarita, are you just going to leave it at that?' Dad hisses.

'Ssh.'

'Don't ssh me, we need to talk. We need to tell her. Swimming's finished. It's over.'

I turn round.

'You can't take that away from me,' I shout. 'It's all I've got left!'

'It's not safe. It could've been you in that hospital. It could've been you who . . .'

'. . . died?'

'Yes.'

'But it wasn't. Look!' I fling my arms out. 'I'm still here. And you can't, won't, stop me swimming.'

'I'm your father, Nicola. I'm telling you . . .'

'I'm sixteen. You can't stop me – unless you get enough people signing up to your petition.'

'What do you mean?'

'Yes, what do you mean?' Mum says.

I can't bottle it up any longer.

'I don't know, Carl, you figure it out.'

'What?'

'You figure it out, Carl.'

'What are you talking about? Why are you calling me that?'

'Because it's your name. Your real name.'

Mum gasps, then there's silence.

Dad staggers back and leans against the wall.

'How did you find out?'

'This.' I open the flap of my bag, take out the folded-up

birth certificate and hold it towards them. 'This is the truth, isn't it? In black and white.'

Neither of them says anything. They look at each other, each waiting for the other to speak.

'I'm not Nicola Anson, I'm Nicola Adams. And you're not Clarke, you're Carl. And you're Neisha.'

'That's who we were, Nic, but not any more,' Mum says eventually. She seems calm now that the dam has burst, whereas Dad is collapsing – curled forward, face obscured, hands squeezing his scalp.

'What happened to telling the truth, Mum?' I say. 'Were you ever going to tell me? And why change your names anyway? What the actual fuck is going on?'

And now Dad explodes. He jumps across the hall and puts one foot on the stairs, shouting, 'Don't you dare use that language in this house! Don't you dare!'

'Why shouldn't I? I don't know what's going on! I don't know who you are or who I am! You're always whispering together when you don't think I can hear. I don't know what the fuck's going on, because neither of you will fucking tell me!'

In two leaps, he's caught up with me on the stairs.

Mum's screaming and pulling at his legs.

'Clarke! Stop it! Calm down!'

And he's grabbed my arms and his face is in my face.

'Everything, everything I do is to protect you. It always has been.'

'Moving? Changing our names? Taking me every-where? Watching me morning, noon and night?'

'Yes, yes! All of that.'

'You can't protect me from life. Shit happens! It just does. I'm suffocating, Dad. You're suffocating me.' I try to escape his grip but he's holding on tight. 'You're hurting me,' I grunt. 'Let go!'

'I can't let go. I can't let you out of my sight. It's close now. The danger. It's getting closer.'

'What danger?'

'The thing that killed Christie.'

'Water?'

'Water.'

'Dad, that just sounds insane.'

Mum's on the stairs now, the three of us squashed together in this narrow space. She puts a hand on Dad's arm.

'Let go, now, Clarke. You don't want to hurt her, do you?'

Again, it's like he's waking up.

'Hurt her . . .? Hurt Nic . . .? No. No, never.'

He moves his hands away from me and I retreat up to the top of the stairs.

'What are we really running from, Dad? What's really going on?'

Looking down at him, wild-eyed and sweating, I wonder if I've known the answer all along. The threat – the thing that I've got to be protected from at all costs – maybe it's here in our house. Maybe it lives within Dad . . . an obsession, some sort of madness.

I leave my question hanging in the hot, stale air of the hallway, and retreat to my room.

SEVENTEEN

'I brought you some food, a little bit of salad.' Mum's voice, right outside my door.

'I'm not hungry.'

'I'd leave it on the floor here, but I don't trust Misty not to have a go at it.'

Sigh.

'Okay, just bring it in.'

She comes into the room, carrying a tray. 'I'll put it on your desk, shall I? I know you probably won't feel like it, but it's here if you do. You should at least drink something. It's lemonade, not . . .'

' . . . not water?'

She nods. 'I'm sorry,' she says.

'What for?'

'Just now. Your dad losing it. Not telling you the

133

truth earlier.'

Without Dad here, the heat's gone out of the argument. Mum's apology reaches out to me and I can't be angry with her.

'Sit down, Mum.'

She sits on the end of the bed. My phone pings. It's been going crazy with people reacting to the news about Christie.

'You've got a text,' she says.

'Yeah, I know.'

'You can look at it, I don't mind.'

'No, it's okay. There's loads of them.' I click the phone into silent mode and put it down.

'About Christie?'

'Yeah. No one can believe it.'

'I'm so sorry. It's very rare for someone to die of water intoxication. She was very unlucky.'

'Water what?'

'Water intoxication. That's what she had. We haven't had a case at the hospital as long as I've worked there. It's very unusual.'

'Her mum said that her brain had swollen.'

'Yes, when you drink too much it can affect your internal organs. Sometimes you can't recover.'

But she'd woken up. She was getting better.

I can't deal with this on my own. I've got to tell someone.

'I did it, Mum. I killed her.'

She looks up sharply, searches my eyes. 'What?'

'She woke up at the end, when I was visiting, and she

asked for some water and I gave her a sip.'

'A sip wouldn't have killed her, baby girl. It wasn't your fault.'

'No, you don't understand. She choked on it. She choked to death.'

She closes her eyes for a moment, then leans forward and takes my hands in hers.

'It was an accident, then, Nic. You didn't kill her.'

'I shouldn't have given her anything. Why didn't I wait for the nurses?'

'Ideally you shouldn't, but you said she asked for it . . .'

'She did. Her lips were so dry. I thought I was helping . . .'

She shuffles up the bed towards me and holds me again, stroking my hair. 'It's okay. It's okay. Ssh . . .'

'What's going to happen?'

'About Christie?'

'About everything. Christie. Dad and that boy with the water pistol. Swimming. Us. Everything.'

'Ssh. You can't worry about everything all at once. It'll be okay.'

'Dad's not okay.'

'No. But he heard today that the boy's family isn't pressing charges. The police just gave him an official warning. It'll be on his record for a while, but that's all.'

'What's going on, Mum?'

'It's his OCD thing. It's got out of control. I'll make him get help, see a doctor. You don't need to worry about it, that's my job.' She sits back a little. 'You've had a terrible shock. Just get through today, and then tomorrow, and the

135

next day. Take it gently. It'll be all right . . . what's that?'

She's looking at the silver chain round my neck. I put my hand to my chest, covering the lump under my T-shirt.

'Just a necklace.'

'You don't wear jewellery, not every day. What is it?'

I keep my hand in place. If she sees it, she'll know I've been going through her things.

'Nothing special.'

But I'm colouring up.

'It is special, isn't it? Has someone given it to you? Are you seeing someone?'

'No!' I try to laugh it off, but it sounds so fake that it has the opposite effect. Her eyes widen with delight. Her mouth forms an O. She leans towards me.

'You've got a boyfriend! Why didn't you tell me?'

Maybe this is my Get Out of Jail card.

'I just . . . it's just early days, you know.'

'Who is it?'

God, who is it? Quick, Nic, think quickly. Mum's staring, shiny-eyed, waiting.

'You don't know him.'

'Okay, so what's his name? Where did you meet him?'

So many questions.

'He's just a boy, Mum, okay? I don't want to give you all the juicy details in case it's nothing.'

'Just his name, then.' She's relentless, and it strikes me that she's been waiting for this moment for a while, like she sees it as a mother-daughter rite-of-passage thing. I get a little twinge of guilt that this longed-for day is nothing but fiction.

'His name . . .' I say. My mind is grappling for a name. Something. Anything. I've got a big, blank space in my head where my quick-wittedness should be right now, coming up with something plausible.

'It's . . . it's Milton.'

The word is out before I've got a chance to stop it. I clap my hand to my mouth, covering the lower half of my face, but it's too late. The stable door is wide open, the imaginary horse has bolted and is kicking up a dust trail in my face.

Mum's face is frozen, then a little frown appears.

'Milton?' she says. 'You mean the same as Milton two-doors-down?'

'Yes . . . the same.' In for a penny. 'Same name. Same person.' I screw up my face, waiting for her reaction.

'Milton?' she says again, and now her hand has gone up to her mouth, but a smile is escaping round the edges.

At the same moment, my phone pings again. We both look at it. Mum's smile gets even wider.

'Look, it's a secret, okay? And we've only just started, so don't say anything, okay? Not to Dad, or anyone.'

Behind her hand she nods.

'You can stop smiling now, it's not a big deal.'

She lowers her hand and tries to pull a straight face. 'Nic,' she says. 'Do you want to talk about anything?'

I look at her, then I get what she means: 'anything' equals 'sex'.

'No! No. Shuttup. Ewww. We've only just started seeing each other . . .'

'Does he know about Christie?'

'I dunno. I haven't told him yet . . .'

'Might be easier to talk to him. It might help.'

'Okay. Secret, remember?'

'I won't tell,' she says. 'Promise.' Then she leans across the gap between us and kisses my forehead, before getting up and leaving the room.

I lean back against my pillows. God, what a mess. Everything's a mess. But Mum's right – I can't sort it all out by sitting here worrying. I close my eyes, but all I can see is Christie's face. The panic in her eyes as she started to choke. Oh, God.

Sweat's dripping down my front, soaking my T-shirt. The air in the room is cloyingly hot. I walk over to the window to see if I can wedge it open a bit further. As I push the handle, my legs press against the radiator and I gasp. It's on, red hot against my bare skin. No wonder this room feels like a furnace.

I crouch down and turn the valve round until it's completely closed. What the hell's the heating doing on anyway?

On the bed, my phone vibrates. I pick it up and scroll through the messages. There are so many, I don't know where to start. Most were sent within the last hour or so, as people heard about Christie. I scroll back through them all, to the one from Harry that came through when I was at the hospital.

Surprise, surprise, he hasn't sent anything since. He must know by now. What's he feeling? The lying, cheating snake. I can't think about him now without feeling sick. What did I ever see in him?

The air is hot and thick. It feels like the oxygen has been squeezed out of it. My room is like a sauna, the walls themselves sweating and sighing. On my desk, the salad Mum brought is already looking wilted and tired.

I don't even try to go to sleep. I strip off and put on some clean pants and a vest top, and sit on my bed, on top of the covers. I don't look at my phone. I don't open my laptop. I sit and stare into space and wait for this horrible day to be over.

The room grows dark around me and still I sit and stare. My eyes start playing tricks on me, seeing colours in the darkness that aren't there. Voices from the street outside sound like they're drifting in from another planet. The people they belong to are aliens – people with ordinary lives, with friends who are all still alive and families who don't have secrets. They've never been scared of their own dad. They're not like me.

The phone vibrates, buzzing over and over again.

The screen flares into life as I unlock it and check my inbox.

Milton.

My imaginary boyfriend.

What does he want?

Nic, you okay?

Yeh. Kind of.

Sorry about Christie. That sucks so bad.

Thnx.

I think I've found the rubber ducky.

?

Click this link.

I open it. It's from a news site, from seventeen years ago. No photos, only text.

LOCAL BOY: DEATH BY MISADVENTURE

Kingsleigh boy, Robert 'Rob' Adams, aged 17, died after an outing to a local beauty spot went tragically wrong. An inquest into his death, on 24th September 2013, heard that he had gone swimming in the Imperial Park lake after school with his younger brother, Carl, and their friend, Neisha Gupta. Ignoring warning signs, the three had been in the lake for a few minutes when they got caught in a violent rainstorm. Carl and Neisha managed to make their way out of the lake, but the body of Robert was found soon afterwards. He had drowned. Mr Oliver Townsend, the coroner, ruled that it was death by misadventure.

I read it twice, then again.
There was a brother.
My dad had a brother.
A brother who drowned.

EIGHTEEN

I read the article again. Of *course* Dad's terrified of water. His brother drowned. And Mum was there too. They were both in it together – this trauma, this terrible, terrible thing.

No wonder he's paranoid about water.

Another message from Milton: *What do you think?*

Explains a lot.

Mm. I reckon.

Why secret tho?

Sad I guess. Too sad.

I put my phone down and lean back again. My eyes are filling up, big fat tears threatening to spill out. Poor Dad. He's lived with this all this time, and it obviously hasn't got any easier. And why should it? How can you possibly cope with losing the person you've shared your childhood with? And it all hurt too much to talk about. Wow.

My phone pings again. I lean over.

More links here.

I'm not sure I need any more. This is it, isn't it? This explains everything. I've been thinking that my dad's going mad, and in a way he has, but he's going mad with grief, a grief he hasn't been able to get over for seventeen years.

I look at the clock. Two forty-three. God, I must have fallen asleep. I'm tired, but not sleepy. I scroll back up to a previous message: *More links here.* Won't do any harm to look. They might help me to understand Dad's story, his experience.

I click on the top one. It's another news article, this time from a few months earlier, a report of the drowning itself. There are pictures this time, the sort of photos that get taken at school — you know, headshots of kids with slicked-down hair and uncertain smiles. One of them's obviously Mum: Neisha Gupta at sixteen. She was beautiful. Smooth black hair, almond-shaped eyes, with a hint of sparkle in them.

The other picture is of two boys: brothers, one a couple of years younger than the other. I look from one to the other and back again. They both look like my dad – the same blue-grey eyes, sloped down at the outside edges, the same square jawline. The younger one is looking to one side of the camera, unsure of himself. The other one, the older boy, is staring straight at the lens. There's something about his expression – he's kind of cocky, like he's winding the photographer up. I'm looking at Dad's brother. Robert 'Rob' Adams, the uncle I never knew.

Except that I do know him.

I've seen his face before. I saw it today.

It's the face of the boy in the pool.

NINETEEN

I stare at the face on the screen. This isn't right. It can't be.

The caption: *Carl Adams, 15 (left) and Robert 'Rob' Adams, 17 (right)*

Dad and his brother. A brother who died in 2013.

My uncle.

Who looks like – who *is*, surely – the boy who visits me underwater.

That's insane – it doesn't make any sense. He died seventeen years ago.

It must be someone that looks like him – maybe a relative, a distant cousin or someone, maybe even his son. That's what my brain is saying, trying to find a logical explanation. But my heart is telling me something different. I know – I've known all along, haven't I? – that this boy isn't like anyone else.

He died before I was born.

He exists underwater.

He's not . . . mortal.

He's something else. An echo of the person he used to be.

My phone blinks off into energy-saving mode. I touch the screen to wake it up, then reach forward and let my thumb trace the shape of his face. The blue-grey eyes stare back at me.

I'm scared now, but also it feels like things are slotting into place. He knew me, didn't he? He used my name when I hadn't told it to him. There was a reason that he found me, not the other girls in the pool. There's a connection. It's starting to make sense in a crazy, screwed-up sort of way.

Maybe I shouldn't feel scared. Maybe I should feel lucky.

We don't have a printer – I don't know anyone who does – but I wish we did. I'd love to print out Rob's picture. Instead, I save the image to my gallery. He'll be there now, whenever I need him.

Sometime, somehow, I've got to have the 'I know you had a brother' conversation with Dad. But can I ever tell him that I've seen him, that he talks to me?

Should I tell Milton about it? How much should I say?

I'm not sure I can tell anyone, say any of this out loud.

I check the clock again. Three-fifty. I need to be up in a couple of hours' time – Saturday morning swimming. Will it even be happening, after what happened to Christie?

My eyelids are feeling heavy. I put my phone on standby and slide down the pillows. I close my eyes, and now, instead of Christie, all I see is the photo from 2013. Blue-grey eyes. Slicked-down hair that's still a bit of a mess. And that look, a kind of *Well? What are you going to do about it?* look.

Rob Adams. My uncle. Somehow frozen in time, as a seventeen-year-old boy.

He's out there somewhere. He's waiting for me in the water.

TWENTY

Early morning. First light making a pale oblong of the window at the end of the pool. A hush in this rectangular space. A moment of peace.

Training was cancelled. None of the other girls are here. And so I can just swim, do the thing that I love, feel normal for a while.

Unbelievably, Harry is at the lifeguard post. He's slumped in the chair, staring across the pool. I stop near the bottom of the ladder.

'What are you doing here?' I say.

He looks down at me, and there's no light, no spark. He could be looking at something on the bottom of his shoe.

'Couldn't sit at home any longer looking at the walls.'

'She was your girlfriend, wasn't she?'

He nods. 'She was the best.'

I thought I could handle this, but I'm stung.

'Gee, thanks,' I say.

'What?'

I look round. No one else is here.

'What about us?' I hiss.

'What do you mean?' He looks genuinely confused. 'There was no "us".'

'All the phone stuff. The photos.'

I can see the truth dawning on him. Maybe now I'll get an apology, or maybe he'll express some guilt over doing the dirty on Christie.

'Oh, that. That was nothing. Everyone does that.'

'I don't believe you. It wasn't nothing to me.'

He smiles and shakes his head.

'It's time somebody grew up. Some people . . .'

'It wasn't nothing! And I had no idea you were seeing Christie. I'd never have—'

'Oh, come on. Everyone knew. Christie couldn't keep a secret to save her life . . .' He stops, realising what he's said, then continues: 'She was the real deal. She was awesome.'

His eyes glaze over and although he's looking in my direction, I know he can't see me. He's seeing Christie, hearing her voice, remembering . . .

I walk towards the deep end with his words ringing in my ears.

That was nothing. Nothing. Nothing.

I don't want to cry. What right have I got? Christie's dead. All that's happened to me is some waste-of-space boy has hurt my feelings. He's not worth crying over. I wipe my arm across my eyes, stand at the edge of the pool, look at the perfect flat water, and dive.

I stretch my body, reaching forward through shades of turquoise. Light filtering through the water. A dark blue highway of tiles between me and the other end.

He's there, beside me. The boy called Rob. He doesn't seem to be moving his arms and legs, yet he swims alongside me, keeping pace, his pale body parallel to mine. He's so close I could almost touch him.

Rob.

You know my name.

I know who you are.

Was. That was a long time ago.

Seventeen years. So why are you here now? What do you want?

I've been looking for you. I've been playing our game, Nicola. Hide-and-seek. Remember?

I don't know what he's talking about. Hide-and-seek?

I found you before, and then I lost you. Someone took you away from me. I've been looking ever since.

What do you want?

I want what's mine. I want what's owing.

His face looms nearer. I can see the pores on his skin, the spots and sores, the streaks of mud.

I don't understand.

Just swim. You belong in the water, Nicola. You belong here with me.

I shouldn't have come here this morning. It feels wrong now, trying to carry on as if nothing has happened. Disrespectful to Christie. And if I hadn't come,

149

I wouldn't have seen Harry. And I wouldn't be talking with my dead uncle. He wouldn't be in my face. Close. Too close.

I want to get out.

You're upset.

I think . . . I think I've made a mistake.

This is your place, Nicola. The water is yours.

I shouldn't have come here today.

Give me those feelings. Give them to me.

Trust me, you don't want them.

Trust me, I do.

I need to breathe.

Who's upset you? Give me their names.

Harry. Mum. Dad.

There's a noise in my ear, a breath, a hiss.

Forget them. You're better than all of them. The best. Just breathe. And swim. Give yourself to the water.

I break the surface, take a long breath in and dip under again. And the more I swim, the better I feel. My limbs feel longer and stronger. There's power in my shoulders and hips.

I cut through the water, lap after lap. Everything else falls away. There's only the physical movement of arms and legs and neck. The rhythm of breathing. Break the surface, breathe in. Under again, push the air out, long and slow.

I swim until the pool starts to fill up with the early-morning casual swimmers: old women and men who have already been awake for hours, walking in the shallows or breast-stroking ponderously to the deep end;

hairy-backed men in too-small trunks and nose clips; professional amateurs who line up a water bottle and a couple of floats at the end of a lane. I don't let any of them put me off. I just plough up and down, hardly feeling my body any more, numb through repetition.

Rob is still with me, but I can't see him. He's quiet now, but I know he's here.

I pause at the deep end, holding on to the side, pushing my goggles on to my forehead. I glance up at the clock. It says eight-forty. That can't be right. I screw up my eyes and look again. I've been swimming for more than two hours! Now that I've stopped my limbs feel heavy in the water. My fingers are pale and corrugated. It's time to get out.

It takes a couple of attempts to pull myself on to the side. I'm just starting to wonder if I'm going to make it when I manage to get the balance of my weight over the lip and I haul my legs out.

Harry's a few metres away, pulling in the lane marker. He'd seen me struggling but didn't offer to help. At the other end the second lifeguard, Jake, is unhooking his end and pulling ropes too. Rope is coiling around Harry's feet. I have to walk past him, or walk the other way round three sides of the pool, and that would look stupid.

The hypnotic calm that I found in the water evaporates. I don't know what to say, what to do. Perhaps I can just get past without saying anything.

'Hey, Nic,' he says when I get close enough for him to talk softly without anyone else hearing. 'What we said earlier. We should just forget about it, yeah?'

'I—'

'No one needs to know about it. Like, it wasn't anything anyway, was it?'

I'm too tired to take any more hurt. I take a step to one side, but he's not done yet.

'So those pictures. You're gonna delete them, right?'

'Oh, yeah. Because you wouldn't want anyone seeing them, would you? You wouldn't want anyone knowing what a two-timing loser you are.'

He's looking at me with undisguised disgust now.

'Do you want *your* pictures on the internet? Do you want me to tweet *them*? Have everybody know what a little whore you are?'

Behind him the water is a choppy mid-blue, stirred up by all those arms and legs. But I can only see red. A red mist of embarrassment and humiliation and fury.

He's the whore. Give him to me.

Rob's voice is in my head.

Without thinking I raise both hands quickly and shove them into Harry's chest. Hard.

And life switches into slow motion. Harry's top half reels away from me. Arms flailing, he takes a step back to try and regain his balance. His back foot is on the edge of the pool. He teeters on the brink for a second or two, his face contorting into a series of comic-book expressions. He seems to be recovering himself. His arms stop wind-milling, and he's still upright – more or less stable – when his feet get whipped from under him. I see him suspended in mid-air, and then his legs hit the water and his head smacks against the tiled edge of the pool.

The noise isn't like anything I've ever heard. I've seen acts of violence on TV and in films, of course, but in real life the sight of it, the sound, is more shocking than you can ever imagine. A rifle shot? A watermelon dropped from a top window? I don't know what to compare it to, but I know I'll never forget it.

He's flopped face-down in the water now. Blood fans out from the wound on his head, like red smoke in the water. His body is surrounded by a tangle of blue rope and orange floats – all in a sea of red.

There are screams from other swimmers. I hear a shout from the far end of the pool. Jake's running round the edge. He dives in halfway along the side, just as I come to my senses and jump into the water next to Harry.

I grab hold of him under his armpits and turn him over. His eyes are open. His mouth is, too. Oh, God.

I pull him up to the side. I can move his body in the water, but out of it, he's too heavy for me to lift. The blood makes him slippery. Blood all down his face. Blood on my hands. Blood pulsing out of him.

Jake's here. ''S'okay, I'll take over now.' He heaves Harry's body up towards the reaching hands on the edge. They pull Harry clear of the water and lay him down. I stare as someone puts their hand on his neck, then leans their head on his chest.

'Is he breathing?' Jake asks.

I turn to look at him, and I'm transfixed by his hands. Why is he wearing gloves? He wasn't wearing them a minute ago. And then his hands find the water and the gloves dissolve. Not gloves, blood. And I look at my hands, resting on the edge of the pool, and I've got red gloves too.

Jake's looking at me now.

'What the hell happened just then?' he says.

But all I can think of is the blood, the blood on my hands, and then everything goes black and I slip under the surface.

TWENTY-ONE

There are hands on me: behind my neck, under my arms, at my waist and my hips. I'm lifted clear and laid flat on my back on the cold, hard tiles. Someone puts something under my feet, lifting my legs up.

'Her eyes are flickering.'

'She's okay. Just a faint. Give her some space.'

I turn over on my side, bringing my legs up as I cough the water out of my windpipe.

Faces looking down on me, shifting in and out of focus. Strangers, Jake and . . . Dad?

I can only have been out for a matter of seconds. I remember it all: Harry falling and cutting his head open. The blood.

I turn my head and Harry's there, lying flat out a few metres away. Someone's found a first-aid kit and is holding a thick pad of white wadding to his head. A dark stain is showing through the layers. His eyes are closed.

'Is he——?' I say.

'What, love?' Dad scrunches up his face and leans closer.

'Is he okay?'

'The ambulance is on its way,' Dad says. He strokes my forehead, over and over. Does he mean the ambulance is on its way for me or Harry? I don't want to be taken off anywhere.

'I'm fine.' I try to sit up.

'Just rest for a little while.'

'No. No, really I'm fine. I want to get out of here.'

Dad helps me to sit up.

'Can we go home?'

'You need to be checked out, but after that, yes, I'm sure. In a little while.'

The people gathered round me start to drift back to Harry. Dad helps me to my feet. 'How are you feeling?'

Truthfully, I feel disconnected, like all of this is happening to someone else. I look down at my fingers. I make them move, clenching and unclenching both fists. I must be here, alive. This must be real. But it still feels like I'm in a dream, or watching a film.

'I'll get a shower,' I say.

'Someone should come with you.'

'I'll come,' a woman nearby says. She's grey-haired, stout, in a flowery costume with a frill of material around her hips. She links her arm through mine, and we start to leave the pool. I catch Jake watching us – me – stony-faced.

The woman, Shirley, helps me fetch my towel and shampoo from my locker. 'Don't lock the door in case you faint again, love. I'll wait outside so no one comes in,' she says.

I push the door to, hang up my towel, put my shampoo bottle down and press the metal button on the opposite wall. The shower starts, running cold for a few seconds, then warm. I step forward, shut my eyes and tip my face into the stream. I squeeze my hands over my head, pushing my hair away from my face, scraping it close to my skull, then – eyes still closed – I peel off my swimsuit and drop it on the floor. I let the water fall on me for a while, like rain, until it dwindles and stops. I reach for the button again, push it, turn round and crouch down. Time to shampoo this day away, get clean.

I open my eyes to see a pair of feet by the door, blocking my way out. Naked feet. Bruised. Marked.

I can see through them, see the tiles he's standing on.

I gasp.

I can hardly bring myself to look up, but I do. Hairy legs with deep scratches in the pale, translucent skin. Wet white boxer shorts clinging to him. Skinny torso, ribs visible. And his face looking down.

Rob.

Hunched over as I am, my naked front is shielded from him by my head and shoulders, knees and shins.

'You shouldn't—You can't—' I stutter.

Ssh. He holds his index finger up to his lips.

'You all right in there?' Shirley shouts.

'Yes. Yes. Just dropped my shampoo.'

In the pool he reads my thoughts.

You can't be in here, I think, making the words as forceful as I can, trying to keep calm.

It's okay.

No! Not like this. It's not right. Please, go away.

Two down, he says. *Two to go.*

What?

We did it. Job done.

I don't understand.

You and me. We solved one of your problems.

Harry? It was an accident. I didn't mean him to hit his head . . .

He got what was coming.

The shower's stopped again. Water trickles down my spine. It drops from my chin on to my knees. And Rob starts to disappear. Everything behind him – the grain of the fake-wood door, the pattern of my towel hanging on the hook – is becoming clearer.

What the——? Where are you going?

Press the button, Nic.

No. I'll see you in the pool. Tomorrow. I'll be there, I promise.

Press. The. Button.

The menace in his voice is unmistakeable.

I can't reach. I uncurl a little and, keeping one hand over my boobs and covering my crotch with my elbow, I reach for the button.

The water rains on to me again and he's back.

Good girl.

I really want to get dry now. I want to go home.

Home. With Mummy and Daddy.

Yes.

Neisha and Carl.

Of course he knows their names, but it still unsettles me to hear him say them.

I've missed them.

Of course you have. They're your family as much as mine. He's your brother. Seventeen years is a long time.

A long time. Coming to an end soon.

What? What is?

The water's running out again.

Rob, I'll see you tomorrow, okay?

He doesn't reply. He just looks down at me and keeps looking. Staring, with his pitiless eyes, at my naked body.

My cubicle door drifts open an inch. I stretch my hand forward to close the gap again.

'Are you nearly done?' Shirley says.

'Yeah.'

The last suggestion of Rob's shape has gone now. I'm alone in the cubicle. I haven't washed my hair, but I don't care. I'm not pressing that button again. Not today.

I stand up and wrap the towel round me.

Shirley's still on guard outside. 'You feeling all right now?' she says.

'Yeah,' I say. I can't put into words how I feel, and if I could, I wouldn't tell anyone.

'So it's okay if I have a quick shower now, while you get dressed?'

'Yeah, sure.'

Someone comes into the changing room and the

159

opening of the door brings a brief burst of noise — the distant wail of an ambulance. Harry on his way to hospital, no doubt. Do they keep the sirens going if someone's died? I don't know how anyone could survive losing that much blood.

He got what was coming.

We did it.

Job done.

It was an accident, wasn't it? Okay, I pushed him. But how could I have known his feet would get caught up in the rope like that? How could I have known he would hit his head?

We did it.

Rob asked me to give him my worries, to tell him who was bothering me. And I did. Mum, Dad and Harry.

Two down, two to go.

Two down — does he mean Christie as well? Oh God. What have I done? What the hell have I got myself into?

Shirley emerges from the shower.

'You haven't made much progress. You all right?'

I look around me. My clothes and toiletries are laid out on the bench, just like they always are.

'Yes. Yes, I'm fine. Bit shaken up.'

'Do you need some help?'

'No, I can manage. Thank you.' I switch on to autopilot, go through my daily routine, until I'm dried and dressed, my hair is brushed and everything's packed away in my bag.

Dad's in the corridor outside the changing room, pacing up and down. As soon as he sees me he rushes over, takes my bag from me and puts his arm round my shoulders.

'Are you all right? Let's get you home. I've rung for a taxi.'

'How did you know I was here? You must have got a text saying training was cancelled.'

'Yeah, and I went back to bed, but when I woke up again and found you were missing, this was the first place I looked. I know you, Nic. I can read you like a book.'

'Are you cross?'

'I was, but when I saw you in the pool and the blood all round you, my heart just stopped. I wasn't angry any more, I just wanted you to be okay.'

'And I am. Except . . . except . . .'

'What is it?'

'Oh, Dad. I'm scared.'

His hand tightens on my shoulder and I bury my head in the curve of his neck. He kisses my hair.

'I was scared too, but it's okay,' he says. 'You're okay now. Let's get you home.'

Maybe he didn't hear me properly, doesn't realise that the fear is still with me.

I think I'm starting to feel what he feels.

I'm scared of what I've done, and what I'm capable of.

I'm scared for him and for Mum.

I'm scared for me.

TWENTY-TWO

I'm lying in bed, the sheets damp around me. Have I slept? I don't know. I was awake when the dawn light started creeping through the crack of the curtains. Awake when the first bird started singing. The air is thick and stifling.

I look at the clock. Nearly six. Normally I'd be up and having a quick snack before training, but not today. I think I'll steer clear of the pool for a little while.

All yesterday, all last night, I had thoughts in my head I couldn't blot out. Christie, Harry. And Rob's voice. *We did it.*

My phone pings. I reach for it and open the new message. It's from Clive.

Team meeting to honour Christie: 8.30 a.m. Swim after. Nic, can you get here for 7.30? Need to talk.

I groan.

Someone taps on the door and immediately opens it. Dad pops his head round.

'Got a text from Clive,' he says.

'Me too. Dad, I don't want to go today. I think I need some time away from there.'

'They'll want to ask you about yesterday. Don't worry, I'll be there.'

'Can I just go after that?'

'I think you've got to go to the team meeting, Nic. Out of respect. Just meet up with them. You don't have to swim.'

I sigh.

'It's that place, Dad. I don't feel safe there any more.'

'I know. But I'll be there. I'll be right with you. Jesus, Nic, it's hot in here.'

'My radiator's been on.'

'What?'

'I can't turn it off.'

'The heating shouldn't even be on. I'll go and have a look at the boiler. You don't need to get up yet. Try and get a little more sleep if you like.'

He closes the door and I close my eyes.

My phone pings again. I reach for it and squint at the screen.

You awake? Milton.

Kind of.

Wanna Skype?

I sit up and reach for my laptop. When I activate Skype, Milton's call request is already there. I accept and two windows open up. Me and him. He's at his desk already, I'm propped up in bed with my hair like a bird's nest and my eyes full of sleep.

'God, I look like a tramp,' I say. I try to smooth my hair down, with only partial success. I wipe my eyes with my scrunched-up hands, making them squeak in their sockets.

'Morning, Nic. You look lovely.'

'Milton, you didn't wake me up just to be pervy, did you?'

He smiles.

'No, I wanted to check you were all right. I heard about Harry.'

'Do you think I did it?' I don't know why I said that. Too sleepy to be careful, I suppose.

'What?'

'Hurt Harry.'

'No! 'Course not.' He frowns. 'Did you?'

'I wanted to. Hurt him.'

'Wow. Why?'

'I thought I liked him, but it turns out he's just a pig. More than a pig. A prick.' I check Milton's reaction. 'Sorry,' I say quickly. 'I shouldn't speak ill of him, not when he's in hospital, but . . .'

'. . . but he is a prick. I could've told you that.'

'Do you know him?'

'He was in my year at school. Tried to flush my head down the toilet in the first year. Nice.'

'God, Milton, I wish I'd known. I would've steered clear.'

'He didn't try to flush you, too, did he?' He's smiling again.

'No. He . . . I can't tell you. I did something I shouldn't have. I didn't know he was . . . and then I pushed him at the pool, I didn't mean to hurt him, just get him wet, but he hit his head. Oh God, can we just talk about something else?'

'Nic, it sounds like an accident. Accidents happen, okay? Either that or you don't know your own strength. I'd better remember that. Anyway, I've been thinking about your dad – and your uncle, the one who drowned.'

Now I'm really awake. For a moment I'd forgotten that Milton knows all about them. Him talking about them makes it all seem more real.

'I don't think that incident is enough to explain how your dad is now. I mean, it's really bad, but lots of people have lost people close to them. There's got to be something more.'

'And is there? Did you find something?'

'A few weeks after the accident, there was a massive flood in Kingsleigh. The river burst its banks and a whole row of houses was flooded up to the second floor. Your mum's was one of them. Your mum and dad both got taken to hospital. You should ask them about it.'

'Yeah. Yeah, maybe I should. My mum doesn't seem freaked by the water, though, Milton. She's just worried about Dad.'

'Perhaps she's the one to talk to, then.'

'Hmm.' Then I remember the last time I talked to her and my face starts to flush. 'Um, Milton, I should tell you something.'

'Yeah?'

'It's a bit embarrassing.'

'Whatever. Shoot.'

'I had to make up a lie really quickly and I just said the first thing that came into my head . . .'

'Yeah?'

'. . . and I kind of ended up telling my mum that we're going out.'

'Huh?'

'I said you were my secret boyfriend.'

He processes my words for a few seconds, then breaks out into a huge grin. God, this is exactly what I was afraid of. Talk about crossed wires. I need to untangle them quickly, before they get in a knot.

'Aw, Nic, you should have said something. You know I like you.'

He's still smiling but I can't tell if there's a serious edge there or not.

'It wasn't . . . I mean, it doesn't mean . . . the thing is . . .'

Now he's properly laughing.

'Hey, Nic. Relax. I like you. I really like you, and I'm flattered that I was the first one to pop into your head, but—'

'It was just one of those things . . .'

'—but I'm pretty sure I'm gay. I mean, I am. Sure. And gay.'

'Oh.'

'Not boyfriend material. Not for you anyway. Sorry.' He holds his hands up in a *What can I do?* kind of gesture.

'Do you mind being my pretend boyfriend, if Mum

asks you?'

'I don't mind at all.'

I breathe a sigh of relief.

'Thanks, Milton. You gave me a locket, by the way. It's really nice.' I fish it out from my vest top and hold it towards the camera.

'Hmm, I've got good taste. Well done me! Who did give it to you?'

'I . . . found it.'

'O-kay. What's inside?'

'Dunno. I can't get it open. It's, like, rusted shut or something.'

'If you open it there might be clues in there as to who it belongs to. You could get it back to them.'

'Yeah, maybe.'

He looks behind him and then back to the screen.

'I think Mum's awake. I'd better see if she's okay. You take care, yeah? No more pushing boys. Stay out of trouble.'

'Okay.'

'See you later, girlfriend.'

'Ouch. See you later.'

The screen goes blank and he's gone and I'm thinking, I could have told him more. I could tell him about Rob.

Rob. The first time I heard him was the first time I wore the locket in the pool. Was that just a coincidence? Milton's right. I should try and get this thing open, look inside. I glance round the room, looking for something to help prise it open.

And then there's a knock at the door.

'Nic, we need to get going in about twenty minutes. Come and have some breakfast.'

The locket will have to wait.

At the pool, there's a reception committee waiting for me. Clive and Jake are there, and one of the managers.

'We need to talk to you about yesterday.'

Dad steps in. 'Will it wait until after training?'

'Afraid not. We'll use the membership room just along the corridor. Nic?'

'I'm coming too,' Dad says.

'Of course.'

The room is just a small office. A couple of desks pushed together. A couple of computers facing each other. No window. It would feel claustrophobic with just two occupants, but with five of us it's more than uncomfortable. There aren't enough chairs.

I'm asked to sit in front of the manager while the others stand. I reach into my bag for my bottle of water and take a swig.

'Nic. I'm Steve, the duty manager. As you know, one of our lifeguards, Harry, was seriously injured here yesterday. I'm looking into the circumstances. Can you tell me what happened?'

'Is he all right? I mean, is he going to be okay?'

'We're waiting to hear how he's doing this morning. They stitched him up yesterday, X-rayed him. He had severe concussion.'

'I'm really sorry . . . I hope . . .'

'I know. Now, in your own words, what happened, Nic?'

'We were just talking after training, mucking about. Messing. He fell backwards, then he seemed to get his balance, but then . . . then he went. I think his legs were tangled in the rope or something. His feet went from under him.'

'Jake here says he saw you push him.'

Jake's standing behind him, arms crossed, face set hard.

Another swig of water to buy myself a little thinking time. A tiny bit trickles out of my mouth. I wipe it with the back of my hand, smearing it across my jaw, and hear a faint whisper close to my ear.

The rope, Nic.

I look round, but no one else has squeezed their way in. It's just the five of us.

'I did . . . just a little push, playing. Messing about, like I said. That's not what made him fall. As I say, we were only having a laugh, and he was getting his balance back from that when his feet went.'

Jake's shaking his head, and then I hear the voice again.

The rope.

'Maybe someone pulled the other end of the rope by mistake. At the other end of the pool.'

I look back at Jake, and so do the others now. His face burns, bright blotches appearing on his neck. 'I didn't pull on it, Steve, I swear to you. No way.'

'Mistakes do happen, though, don't they?' I say, innocently. 'Everyone makes mistakes.'

'That's not what happened. You pushed him. Shoved him. I saw it.'

He's shouting now, his voice too loud for the room, his

frame seeming to get bigger and more threatening by the second.

'All right, all right.' Clive's squaring up to him, putting his body between me and Jake. And now Dad's jumping in.

'You heard her. It was the rope. She should know. She was nearest.'

'Dad, it's okay.'

He's got his hand on my shoulder, gripping hard, the sweat from his palm soaking through. 'You need to think about the health and safety here.' He shoves an accusing finger towards Steve's face. 'First Christie and now this! What sort of place are you running? How can I be sure my girl is safe?'

'Dad, for goodness' sake, calm down.'

'Now, just one minute,' says Steve. 'We take health and safety very seriously here. There's no suggestion that Christie's illness had anything to do with—'

'That's two now. Two carted off from here in an ambulance. Do you think that's safe? 'Cause I don't.'

They're all on their feet now, shouting across the table. I slip out from under Dad's grip and make for the door. I pause outside, leaning against the wall and listen to them. Eight o'clock in the morning and I'm drenched with sweat. I need a drink. I need to cool off.

I could leave now, but even this early it would be like stepping into an oven. Even though I'm scared, the thought of that rectangle of water is too strong. A relatively cool body of water. My body immersed in it.

I walk along to the changing room.

TWENTY-THREE

Half an hour before the team is due to meet. So twenty minutes to swim, to switch off and stretch and cool down. No Harry on the lifeguard's perch. No Christie in the pool. But Rob will be in there. Do I really want to do this?

I look at the water. There are some early morning swimmers making the water a little choppy. A couple of lanes are roped off and empty. A board on the side says, *Closed for training*. Whether it was meant to be for the swimming team or lifeguard training, there's nobody there now, and it's got to be better than dodging the flying elbows in the public 'fast lane'.

I sit on the edge and ease myself in.

No body under the water. No voice.

Perhaps he'll leave me alone now. I can have the

meditative swim I really need. Just me and the water.

I launch in, savouring the split second when I give myself to the water, trusting it to meet me, support me, hold me. And it does. It takes me in and I stretch and move forward.

And he's here.

I can't see him, but I can feel him.

Rob.

He's close. Too close.

Feels good, doesn't it?

What?

Winning. Christie and that boy. Dealt with. Out of the way. Punished.

I didn't mean them to . . . I didn't want . . .

Yes you did. You know you did.

No! Not like that.

But you made it happen, Nicola.

He's right, isn't he? I gave Christie the water. I pushed Harry.

We did it together. You and me. We're a team.

I want it to stop.

Soon. Two to go, remember?

Mum and Dad. I gave him their names when I was mad at them.

I didn't mean it. I was just cross, confused. I don't want to hurt them.

Don't you? They lied to you, Nicola. They want to control you.

They're just trying to protect me. I don't want them hurt.

You don't know them.

Of course I do. I live with them. They've looked after

172

me for sixteen years, loved me.

Sixteen years of lies. Running from the truth.

I don't understand. I don't understand why you're here, what you want. I'm going to get out now. I can't handle this any more. I want it all to stop.

I'm nearly at the far end of the pool. I kick harder, reach for the side.

It wasn't an accident. It was murder.

Stop it! I don't want to hear any more. They're my mum and dad. I love them.

Bring them back to me in the water. We've got unfinished business.

I grab the edge of the pool and lift my head out of the water. I'm breathing hard. Around me, everyone else is having a normal Sunday swim. They have no idea of the nightmare that's playing out next to them. As I look at them ploughing up and down, at the mums and dads with their toddlers in the shallow end, I find it hard to believe this is real.

Am I having a breakdown? Is this just in my head? It must be. Rob died seventeen years ago. How can he be here?

Still holding the side, I dip my head under.

His voice is so close, it feels like he's inside me.

You owe me, Nicola. Bring them back to me, or there'll be more blood on your hands.

I pull myself up, break the surface, put both hands on the edge and lever myself out of the water. Once on my feet, I shake my head, then smooth the water off my arms and legs with my hands. I wish I could scrape his voice out of my ears, erase the sight of him from my memory.

I walk back to the changing room. The team meeting is due to take place in the café by reception in a few minutes time. No time to shower again, and I wouldn't anyway, not after last time. I get changed quickly, put my stuff in my bag and go to find the others.

I'm the last to arrive. They're sitting round a couple of tables that have been pulled together. Clive's standing nearby. I can't see Dad.

When he spots me, Clive takes me aside. 'Your dad's outside. We had to ask him to leave. He got very . . . aggressive.'

My ears are still ringing from Rob's threats. And I suddenly wonder: does Dad take after Rob, or is Rob like Dad? Two brothers with a temper, an intimidating edge. Must run in the family.

'God. I'm sorry,' I say. 'He's been on edge recently.'

'Well, he's banned now. Sorry, Nic. We have to take the safety of the staff and other customers seriously.'

'Of course. He wouldn't hurt anyone, though, he's just . . . it's okay. I understand.'

We join the others. There isn't an empty space. No one shuffles up to make room for me. I take a chair and set it outside the group.

'Come on, girls, shuffle up so Nic can come in.'

Glances are exchanged round the table. There's a long, long pause until finally one of them moves sideways, creating a not-quite-big-enough gap. I move my chair forward, but I'm still not part of the circle.

'Okay,' Clive says, 'thank you all for coming. I know this is a very difficult time but I wanted us to get together to remember Christie, share our memories of her, share our feelings – maybe have a swim together. I know it's not easy, but I also know that this team meant the world to her and she'd want us to stick together, support each other, work together to get through this. Does anyone want to say something?'

A couple of the girls are crying. No one wants to talk.

'Okay, well, I'll start things off. For me, Christie was one of those girls a coach like me dreams of finding. She had a gift, a natural ability, but she was also prepared to put the work in – and, more than that, she was devoted to her team. I feel blessed to have known her. I can't believe that she's gone . . .' His voice breaks. His eyes are red-rimmed and he turns his head away, embarrassed at his show of emotion.

Pretty much everyone is crying now. I can feel a lump in my throat, tears pricking behind my eyes, but I can't let them out.

'I know I'm the newest one on the team,' I say, 'but I just wanted to say—'

'Don't, Nic,' Nirmala cuts in.

'Don't what?'

They're all looking at me now.

'Don't say anything. You shouldn't even be here, should you?'

'What do you mean? I'm part of this team, I was Christie's fr—'

'Don't say you were her friend. You weren't her friend. You should never have given her that water—'

'Now, Nirmala, let's calm things down, okay?' Clive says,

175

but the others are nodding and muttering in agreement.

'And what was that with Harry yesterday? He'd just lost his girlfriend and you pushed him. What the hell was that about?'

'I can explain. I—'

'Don't bother. We don't want to hear it. You're not wanted here. *Christie* wouldn't want you here.'

I look round the group, trying to catch someone's eye, find an ally. No one will look at me. Clive holds both hands out, palms up, and shakes his head.

I scrape back my chair and stumble out of the café, on through the exit door and on to the concrete walkway, my vision made blurry by the tears that have finally burst through.

Dad's waiting outside. 'What happened? Where were you?'

I sniff hard, try to take a breath.

'I had a quick swim, then I went to the team meeting.'

He looks at his watch.

'The others are going swimming,' I say, 'but I've had enough.'

'Yeah, I reckon I've had enough of this place, too. Let's go home.'

He offers me a tissue and we walk along together.

'They think I did it, Dad.'

'Did what?'

'Killed Christie. Put Harry in hospital. The other girls think I did both those things.'

He stops walking and I mirror him. He holds my arms, just below the shoulders. His palms are clammy on my bare skin. Beside us, traffic passes close by, adding hot fumes to the thick, warm air.

'They were accidents, Nic. Accidents happen.'

'Like all those girls?'

'What?'

'The ones on the news. The ones who died in water. Do you think they were just accidents?'

'Your mum does. But I'm not sure. Actually, I don't think they were accidents at all. I think there's a pattern.'

So do I. Christie. Harry. All those girls. I know what Rob's capable of. Maybe he did it himself . . . or maybe he had help from someone like me.

'But what you're talking about – Christie and Harry – that's different. You mustn't beat yourself up about them.'

'I feel . . . responsible.'

'No. No, it's not your fault. Okay, it was silly to push Harry, but you didn't mean him any harm. And you were trying to help Christie, do what she asked you . . .'

'The girls hate me.'

He ruffles my hair. 'They're all in shock, grieving. They'll come round. Just give them time.'

'Do you ever get over stuff like this? Can you?'

'Yes, love. It feels like things will never get better, but they do.'

'You'd know, I suppose.'

'Huh?'

'I know about your brother, Dad. I know you had a brother who died.'

He puffs his cheeks out, then exhales all the air he has in him. He leans forward and props himself up, bracing his hands on his thighs.

'You must miss him. Why don't you ever talk about him?'

Dad still can't talk. I put my hand on his back. The sweat from his back soaks through his T-shirt, making a hand print where I've touched him.

'It was a long time ago,' he says eventually.

'Seventeen years.'

'Yeah.'

'And it still knocks the breath out of you. So maybe it's not so easy to get over things.'

He looks up at me.

'I've tried to forget him, Nic. That's all I want to do. Forget him and move on.'

'Why? He was your brother.'

'He . . . I . . . we did things . . . things I'm not proud of. He was . . . a dangerous person.'

Sixteen years of lies.

I shiver.

'What happened to him? I've seen some articles online. Are they right? Was it an accident?'

'Yeah. An accident. We were messing around, and then the weather turned and your mum and I got out of the lake . . . and Rob didn't.'

Messing around. That's what I told everyone I was doing with Harry. A story for public consumption – a lie.

Is this what this is? Is my dad spinning the story of the past so it suits him better?

It wasn't an accident. It was murder.

TWENTY-FOUR

The bus is achingly slow as it winds its way through the suburban shopping streets. At last we reach our stop. Mum, Dad and I hurry through the pedestrian entrance, past the large iron gates and down the long sweeping drive, walking as fast as we can in our Sunday best. Dad's in his interview suit, Mum and I in black dresses. I've borrowed a pair of shoes from Mum – black patent court shoes that are pinching my feet. They clip-clop like horses' hooves on the tarmac. I wish I could take them off.

The other mourners are gathered outside the chapel, waiting for their turn to go in. Through a shabby trellis, with a dried-up rose clinging to its fretwork, I can see the guests from the previous ceremony filing out of the back door, pausing to read the cards on a row of wreaths laid flat on the floor.

Nirmala, Shannon and the others from the team are standing in a group. Jake's there, too. They're held together with arms linked or draped across shoulders. Tight.

One of the girls clocks me as I approach. I can read her lips. 'She's here,' she says to the others. Some turn round and stare. Nirmala and Shannon keep their eyes firmly on the ground, still giving me the cold shoulder. I'm not going to let them.

I break away from Mum and Dad and try to join the group. 'Hi,' I say.

Nobody answers.

Perhaps they didn't hear.

'Hi,' I try again.

Nirmala tears her eyes away from the ground, but can't bear to meet mine. She looks past me, to where my parents are standing. Her cheeks are flushed, eyes unnaturally bright.

'Don't start, Nic,' she says. 'Don't talk to us.'

'Nirmala, I didn't mean to hurt her. I gave her a tiny sip, because she asked me to.'

'I can't believe you're here. You've got a nerve.'

'I keep telling you, I never meant to hurt her. She was my friend—'

'You weren't her friend and you're not ours. We don't want you here.'

A long black vehicle is coming down the drive towards us.

'You might not like it, but I'm part of the team, you

can't push me out.'

'You did that yourself, you slag, when you sent that picture to Christie's boyfriend.'

It feels like the ground's falling away beneath my feet. They've seen it – the photo on Harry's phone.

'He's sent it to you? He's better?'

'Well, he's conscious, anyway. I saw him in hospital yesterday,' Jake says. 'He gave me his phone, asked me to look after it.'

'It's not what it looks like,' I splutter. 'I didn't know he was seeing Christie. I didn't—'

'Just stop it, Nic. Stop right there. Have you no respect? She's here,' Nirmala says.

The hearse draws to a halt opposite the entrance to the chapel. The other mourners are filing in. The girls follow, arms around each other, and I'm left standing, looking at the coffin sitting in a sea of tributes in the back of the hearse, like a trophy in a glass display case.

Mum touches my elbow.

'We'd better go in. Are you okay?'

'Yes,' I say, numbly, and I let her and Dad gently guide me in through the chapel doors and into a pew at the back.

The service passes in a blur. Pretty much everyone is crying. The order of service says it's meant to be a celebration of her life, but grief has won the day. Shock, hurt and disbelief at a life cut so tragically short.

I want to be like the others. I want to cry for Christie, share the grief with them. But my eyes stay obstinately dry. And while half of me is listening to the vicar, the readings, the poems, the prayers, the other half is churning with resentment and shame.

All the girls know. Soon everyone in this chapel will know. My mum. My dad. The whole city will know. I'm the girl who sexted Christie's boyfriend. I'm the slag who betrayed her.

Slag. Bitch. Whore.

There's no point denying it. After all, I did send the pictures. I can try saying that I didn't know Christie and Harry were seeing each other, but I don't think anyone's in the mood to listen. I'm guilty in their eyes. I'm beneath contempt.

Towards the end of the service there's a bit of commotion in the pew occupied by the swimming team. Shannon, overcome with emotion, sits down heavily during the last hymn. She curls forward in her seat while the girls either side rub her back and fan her.

And now the final act. The vicar intones as curtains slides around the coffin. This is the end.

There's a shout as Shannon slips on to the floor. Her parents rush forward. Another girl sinks to her knees.

I think of Milton's verdict of the girls in school. Mass hysteria. Perhaps this is another case of it. I don't feel faint or queasy this time, but Mum squeezes my hand.

'You okay?' she whispers.

'Yeah.'

'I expect it's just a bit much for them. I'm going to help. You stay with Dad.'

She bustles forward and is soon lost in the throng. The whole thing's descending into chaos. At least I can escape before everyone's remembered about me and my crimes.

'Dad, can we wait outside?'

He nods. We're meant to file out of the other door, but we'd have to pick our way through the knot of people at the front, so instead we just leave by the entrance. There's another huddle of mourners waiting for the next funeral on the conveyor belt. We make our way through them and walk around the side of the chapel to the back garden to wait for Mum.

But she doesn't come out. Hardly anyone does. The conveyor belt has jammed. An older couple, maybe Christie's grandparents, emerge and stand in the shade. Dad wanders up to them.

'What's going on?' he asks.

'They're going down like ninepins in there,' the old chap says. 'There's something wrong with the girls.'

By now I can hear the wail of an ambulance floating through the clammy air, see a flashing light speeding along the top road, the other side of the cemetery wall. It turns into the site and heads down the drive. It's followed by two more.

'God, Dad, what's happening?'

I start to run towards the door, but he grabs me. 'Don't go in there.'

'They're my friends!' *Were* my friends.

'You'll just be in the way. Let the professionals deal with it. Don't get hot and bothered.'

'I'm already hot.' The afternoon sun is frizzling the skin on the back of my neck. 'Have you got a drink?'

'Yeah. Come and stand in the shade.'

The edge of the roof is creating a line of shade along the wall of the chapel. I lean back and swig from Dad's water bottle.

'Just a little. Sip it, Nic.'

But I can't sip. My mouth is parched. I gulp the stuff down, tipping my head back so I can get it down my neck.

Dad grabs the bottle from out of my hand and it splashes my face. And I hear a voice. Rob's voice.

It's all for you, Nic. Nasty girls. Bitches.

'Dad!'

'That's enough, Nic. Remember where you are,' he whispers. 'What happened.'

Ignore him. His time's up, Nic. Bring him back to me. Do it, or the killing will carry on.

I look round. Of course he's not here. How could he be?

But somehow he is. He's with me.

And I shudder as I realise: he's with me wherever I go. He was looking for me and he found me, and now he won't let me go.

I close my eyes tight shut. I visualise the word NO in capital letters. I want this to stop. I don't want to be part of it any more.

NO, I think, sending the message to Rob as strongly as I can without saying it out loud. NO. NO MORE.

'You all right, Nic?' Dad asks.

I open my eyes again.

'Yeah,' I say. 'Just too hot. Dad, do you believe in ghosts?'

He looks at me sharply.

At that moment Mum comes out of the chapel door. She strides up to me and puts her hand on my forehead. 'How are you feeling, Nic?' she says.

'I'm fine. A bit hot, that's all.'

'Let's get you home.'

'What's going on in there?'

'It's the whole team. They've all got fevers. Some of them are having difficulty breathing. Looks like it could be something like legionella to me.'

'What's that?'

'I'll tell you later. I'm going to ring for a taxi.'

In the taxi, Mum keeps watching me like a hawk, but I don't feel any different. Just hot, but everyone's hot.

'What's legionella, Mum?'

'It's a bacteria. It can make you quite poorly.'

'Kill you?'

She pauses. 'Sometimes. If you're old or ill. Not young people like you.'

'Never?'

'Not usually.'

'How do you catch it?'

'Through water,' Dad says. 'You inhale it in water droplets or fine spray.'

Now I do feel sick.

'Is that right, Mum?'

'Yes, it lives in water tanks and air-conditioning systems, that sort of thing.'

'Swimming pools?'

'They're treated. Should be safe. But it might be in the air-con or the showers.'

'But if it's the whole team . . .'

'Except you. You're all right, aren't you?'

'Yes. I think so.'

'I wonder why you're different.'

I think about my last swim. I was too scared to get in the shower afterwards. And I didn't swim with the others. Presumably their routine afterwards was the same as usual.

'I didn't have a shower,' I say. 'The last time I swam. Do you think that's it?'

Mum gets her phone out and rings the hospital. She tells them what I've said.

'They'll test the water there. They'll have to. They'll probably close the pool until the tests come back.'

'Close the pool?'

'It's a serious public health issue, Nic. They won't have a choice. I'm sorry.'

'No. No, it's fine. I was going to tell you, I want a break from it anyway.'

'Swimming?' Dad says.

'Yeah. It's just got too much.'

He puts his arm round me. I don't want him to say anything smug or triumphant, and he doesn't. He doesn't say a word. I rest my head on his shoulder until we get home.

TWENTY-FIVE

The bathroom door resists a little as I turn the handle and push against it. Then it gives and I'm in. Mum's already in there.

'No!' she yelps.

She's sitting on the edge of the bath, naked.

I've seen her like this before, of course, but not for years. It's a shock for us both. She doesn't try to cover herself up – we've never been particularly shy of each other in our family – but she does look ashamed.

'I'm sorry, I'm sorry,' I shout. I'm halfway out of the door again when my brain starts to register what I've seen. I stop.

'Mum? What are you doing?'

'I'm . . . I'm washing myself.'

'But you're not, are you?'

There's no water in the bathtub. The shower isn't on. She's got a wet wipe in her hands. She was using it to clean under her armpit as I walked in. Wiping herself clean, not washing.

'Can we talk about this in a minute? Please. I'll come and find you. Just close the door now.'

I retreat and pull the door to. For some reason I feel dirty too now. I want to wash these feelings away. Instead, I go into my bedroom and sit on the bed. A few minutes later, she joins me. She's got a thin summer dressing gown wrapped round her.

'Nic,' she says. 'You could try knocking next time.'

'I didn't think anyone was in there. You could try locking the door.'

'I did. Well, I thought I did. That catch has always been a bit dodgy.'

'Okay, I'm sorry. I didn't mean to . . . I mean I wouldn't have . . .'

'It's okay.'

We sit in silence for a minute, pondering the gap between our words and reality.

'So . . .?' I say, as in *What the hell did I just walk in on?*

'I just . . . couldn't be bothered to run a bath.'

'Or take a shower?'

'Or take a shower.'

'Or use soap and water in the basin?'

'Those wipes are refreshing when it's so hot.'

'Or . . . or you're as freaked out about water as Dad is.'

She looks at me then, and her eyes are haunted. She's looking away – looking down, left, right – anywhere but at me. Her hand goes up to her ear and plays with the earlobe.

'Mum, don't even bother lying any more. You told me that it's always better to tell the truth. Tell me the truth now. Are you scared of water?'

She closes her eyes, takes a few deep breaths.

'Yes, I'm scared. I don't want your father to know. He's so close to the edge right now. I keep trying to reassure him, calm him down. I don't want this getting out of hand.'

It's Rob. They're both scared of what the water is harbouring, but neither of them will say it, use his name. Is this the moment to tell her that I know?

'What is it? Why are you so scared? What are you scared of?'

'A long time ago, before you were born, water nearly killed me twice.'

'The lake. I've . . . um . . . seen the articles on the web.'

'The lake, yes. And afterwards there was a flood. It destroyed Grandpa's old house. I was inside.'

'You never said. There seems to be a lot I don't know.'

'It was before your time. History.'

'I still don't understand. You haven't been scared for seventeen years, have you?'

'Yes and no. When you've been through that sort of thing, it never really leaves you. It's always there.'

'That's not it, though. You haven't been like this all the time. Using wipes instead of water. We used to have baths together, remember? When I was little . . .'

There's doubt in her eyes. She's weighing up whether to tell me the truth or not.

'You think there's something evil in the water, don't you? Just like Dad.'

She bites her bottom lip.

'I think there could be. I think we all need to be careful. You, me, him. Nic, if you ever see anything – anyone – in the water who shouldn't be there, you must tell me. Come to me, not Dad.'

Anyone. Can I tell? Should I?

'Mum. There's a boy at the pool . . .'

'A boy? A boy you like?'

'No, not exactly . . .'

'I thought you were seeing Milton. He's a nice boy, Nic. Don't play games with him, not that sort of game. Don't mess him about. If you're not serious about Milton, then don't string him along. He's very sensitive and he's got a lot on his plate.'

'I know. I'm not . . . it's not like that . . .'

The bedroom door opens and Dad walks in, carrying a handful of tools and a washing-up bowl. He takes in the scene.

'What's this? A girls' pow-wow? Am I interrupting?' He doesn't wait for an answer. 'I can't turn the boiler off. It's gone crazy, it's like it's possessed. I'm going to drain the system. If I take the water out, that'll stop it.'

He marches over to the radiator.

'Shouldn't you get a plumber?' Mum says. 'If it's still on, if it's still trying to heat something that isn't there – isn't that dangerous?'

'Nah, it'll be fine. No need to shell out a hundred quid for a call-out. I can do it myself.'

'You're not a plumber, Clarke.'

'I've worked on enough building sites, Sarita. I know what I'm doing. Stop fussing. Anyway, what were you girls talking about?'

'Nothing,' we say together. Then we look at each other, like we've been caught out, but Dad's too busy with the job in hand to notice. He kneels down, places the bowl under one end of the radiator and starts trying to undo a rusted-up nut with a spanner. He grunts with the effort.

'Never mind,' he says. 'Can you go and look for some more containers — buckets or big plastic tubs? I'm going to do all the rads. This has gone on for long enough. If I get the water out, out of the whole system, it'll be better for everyone.'

Mum and I go off in search of buckets.

'He'd be better off taking out the fuse, or disconnecting the boiler from the electricity, wouldn't he? That would stop it working.'

'Oh, let him just get on with it. At least he's busy, not staring at that computer screen, and he's off your case for a bit.'

'It's the water, isn't it?' I say. 'He wants to get rid of the water.'

Mum doesn't reply. She pokes around in the cupboard under the sink. 'I think there are some buckets in the shed, Nic. Can you go and look? While you're in there, can you get the barbecue out? Think it would do us all good to do something a bit different. You could invite Milton, if you like . . .' There's a little smile playing at the corner of her mouth.

'Mu-um . . .'

'I'm only kidding. Unless you do want to invite him . . .'

I'm out of the kitchen and out of earshot before she can embarrass me any further. Misty trails after me. She has a quick sniff round the shed until I chase her out, remembering the time she managed to knock over a tin of white paint and paddle it all through the house. While I lock up the shed again, she flops into a patch of shade underneath one of the bushes in the border.

The rest of the day feels almost normal. Dad's busy inside. Mum and I set up the barbecue and the sunshade and make some salads. She sends me to the corner shop to buy some buns and a packet of frozen burgers. I'd normally take Misty with me but the sun is still punishing, its heat radiating up from the pavement. I leave her lying under the bush, tongue lolling out, panting hard.

The bottom of my flip-flops are turning tacky, starting to melt. It makes walking a bit difficult. I could take them off, but I'm worried about burning the soles of my feet.

Milton's coming out of the shop as I go in. He holds the door for me.

'Hey, girlfriend,' he says.

'Hey,' I say, blushing.

'Tough day.'

'Yeah. Did you hear about the girls on the team?'

'It's all over Twitter. Are you okay?'

'Yeah. Think so.'

Milton closes the door and guides me gently round into the shade of the shop canopy. We lean against the wall.

'Nic,' he says. 'I'm starting to think your dad's on to something. There's too much happening. I think there's some weird shit going on.'

'I know,' I say.

'You think so too?'

'There is something . . .'

'So . . .?'

'I can't tell you.'

''Course you can. You can tell me anything.'

'It's crazy.'

'That's okay . . . Crazy's okay. I deal with crazy every day. Come on, Nic, spill . . .'

I don't know where to start, what to say. I run through it in my head, but the words won't come.

'Is it about your dad?'

'Yes. No . . . it's about me.'

I feel like I might actually break in two, split down the middle, if I say it out loud. It doesn't seem possible that I can tell someone what's going on and still live and breathe like a normal human being. Because this isn't normal. None of it is normal.

'I can see my uncle. The dead one. He's doing things . . . making me do things . . . bad things.'

'What do you mean?'

'I see him in the water. He found me in the swimming pool. And since then . . . things have been happening.'

'What things?'

'I . . . I gave Christie the sip of water that killed her. I pushed Harry.'

'And he . . . he made you do it?'

'Yes! No. I don't know. He understands my feelings. He can read my thoughts. It's like . . . those girls were really mean to me, they pushed me out, made me feel bad . . . and now they're in hospital.'

'But that's like a bug or something. You didn't do that.'

'I think he did. I think the bug that's making them ill was in the water at the pool.'

Milton rolls his head back against the wall and breathes out slowly.

'Holy shit.'

'Do you believe me?'

He opens his eyes again and turns his head. A little trickle of sweat makes its way down the side of his nose. I hardly dare to look at him, but I need to know. Does he think I'm mad? Is he on my side?

His brown eyes search mine. I think of all the times I've been mean to him, all the put-downs. He could crush me now, if he wanted to.

He pushes his glasses up a little, licks the salt sweat off his top lip.

'I believe you, Nic,' he says. 'I do believe you.'

It's too hot for hugs. Instead, I slip my sticky hand into his. He gives it a little squeeze.

'But you mustn't tell, okay? Dad's pretty much having a breakdown right now. And Mum . . . Mum's scared too. They're both . . . I've never seen them like this. So please, please, Milton, don't say anything. Okay? I'm handling it.'

'How exactly are you handling this? What are you going to do?'

'I don't know.'

'You're not on your own, okay? Don't think you're on your own.'

'Thanks.'

'And whatever you do, you need to be careful, really careful. I want you to be okay, Nic.'

We stand for a little longer, hand in hand, backs against the wall. Then, he waits for me while I get the things on Mum's list and we walk home together. He carries my shopping as well as his.

'Do you want to come for tea? Anson family barbecue?'

'Or Adams family?'

'God, yeah. Sounds more appropriate somehow. Want to be part of our little freak show? And your mum, too?'

'Mum won't come. I'd better stay in with her.'

'You sure?'

'Yeah.'

'There's plenty of burgers . . .'

'Nah, that's okay. Another time maybe. I've got some stuff to do anyway. Going to google "ghostbusting", see what I can come up with.'

I can't tell if this is one of his jokes or not. He hands me my shopping bag.

'Skype me, okay?' he says. 'Or text me. I've always got my phone on me. Day or night.'

'Okay. Thanks.'

I watch him as he turns into his front garden and shambles up the path. By the door, he turns round. 'Stay safe, girlfriend.' This time he's smiling, and it brings an answering smile out in me.

I can see a plume of grey smoke tufting into the sky over the roof of my house. I walk round the side and let myself through the gate into the back garden. Dad's poking at the charcoal on the barbecue with some tongs. He's just wearing his shorts, a baseball cap and some old slippers. He's got a beer open on the fold-up table beside him.

Mum walks out of the house carrying a couple of bowls of salad. 'You don't need to keep poking it,' she says.

'Hey, I know what I'm doing. Man make fire. Man cook,' he says, beating his bare chest with his free hand balled up in a fist.

I can't help smiling again. This is Dad how I remember him when I was little. How our family used to be. Can we really be like this again? Maybe we can.

'Yes, all right. Well, start cooking those sausages, then. Woman hungry,' Mum says. I pass Dad the packet, then sit down and start to split the buns in half and pile them on a plate.

TWENTY-SIX

I spot Misty's back legs sticking out from behind the bed.
'Ooh, you're in trouble,' I say. 'Everyone's looking for
you. There's a sausage with your name on it downstairs.'
No need to tell her it's one that fell off the grill and on to
the ground. 'What are you doing here?'

The sound of my voice normally triggers a ridiculously
over-enthusiastic response in her. She should be round my
legs now, jumping up. Hell, even the sound of my foot-
steps would usually be enough. But it's hot, crushingly
hot. No wonder she's listless – I'm sapped of energy too.

I flop down across my bed and peer over the side. The
washing-up bowl at one end of the radiator has a couple
of inches of rusty brown water in it. Misty isn't moving.
She's lying on her side. The patch of carpet around her
head is dark and wet.

'Misty?' I say. She doesn't raise her head. Her ear doesn't twitch, and her eyes stay fixed and glassy. I reach down and touch the fur on her back. She feels normal – the body beneath isn't stiff or cold – but it isn't moving either. There's no rise and fall of her ribs, no quivering in her muscles as she chases squirrels through her dreams.

'No, no, no, no, no, no,' I say, as if denying it can somehow make it not true. 'Please, no. Don't do this.'

I climb off the bed and kneel down next to her on the floor.

'You can wake up now. It's all right. No one's cross at you. It's okay to be here. Just wake up.'

I touch her muzzle, the meltingly soft black skin around her mouth. There's no hot breath from her nose or mouth. Nothing. The skin is damp, a bit sticky. The last thing she did was to throw up. Then she simply lay in her own mess, and was gone.

I look at the washing-up bowl. It looks as though Misty had been drinking the evil-looking water.

'Mum! Dad! Muuuummm!'

It seems obscene to make so much noise in this place – the place where Misty is lying – but I can't help it. I lean over her, my tears dripping on to her side, a string of saliva escaping from my mouth.

Mum and Dad rush upstairs.

'What is it? What's—? Oh my God!'

'Is she—?'

They join me on the floor.

'We should get her to a vet,' Dad says. He starts to ease his hands under her body.

Mum shakes her head. 'She's gone. She's gone.'

'But what's—? Why—? What's all that wet stuff round her head? Oh my God, the water. The water from the radiator. I left it draining. It's got that stuff in it, to clean it out . . .'

'You weren't to know. She shouldn't have been in here. She's not – she wasn't – allowed upstairs.'

'Of course I should have known! I should have shut the door. He's killed her. He's killed Misty. Right here! In Nic's room!'

He grabs the washing-up bowl and throws the whole thing out of the window. I hear the plastic snap as it lands in the front garden below. He leans on the windowsill and his shoulders start to shake. He's crying.

Mum stands up and goes over to him. She puts her hand on his back and moves it gently up and down his spine. 'Ssh, Clarke. You'll upset Nic. This is bad enough without—'

'I know,' I say. 'I know about Rob.'

They both turn round and stare at me.

'That's the "he" you're talking about, isn't it? The "he" you're so scared of. I know who "he" is.'

'What do you mean?'

'Don't pretend. Please. Stop lying to me. You had a brother, Dad, who drowned in a lake seventeen years ago, but, somehow, he's back. He's back and he's killed . . . killed . . .' I can't bring myself to say her name.

Neither of them says anything. They simply stand and gape at me. A couple of hours ago, I swore Milton to secrecy, but it doesn't seem to matter now. Nothing matters.

'I've seen him. He was at the pool. In the water. He spoke to me.'

Mum gasps. Dad grips the edge of the windowsill. His knuckles are white.

'I knew it,' he breathes. 'I knew he was back.'

Mum shushes him. 'Be quiet. Let her speak, tell us what she knows. Go on, Nic.'

'He says he has . . . unfinished business.'

Telling Mum and Dad should be a relief, but it feels unreal. I'm kneeling here in my own room, with my dog dead in front of me and my parents shocked and scared, and I'm telling them about the ghost who killed her. I move my fingers in Misty's fur, feel her softness, watch how the waves and curls of hair move in response to my touch. Evidence to my senses that this is real, after all. But it still feels like a movie, like I'm watching someone else's life, or living in someone else's dream, nightmare.

I extract my fingers from Misty's fur and pinch the skin on the palm of my hand hard, squeezing a tiny section between the nails of my thumb and index finger. My brain registers a sharp point of pain. I squeeze harder. The pain increases, but I still feel disconnected.

'Is he here? He's here, isn't he?' Dad says. 'Can you see him? Can you hear him?' He looks wildly round the room.

I still feel like a witness, like everything here is on the other side of a thick glass window. I force myself to respond. 'No. I can't see him. He's not here now. I don't think he is, anyway.'

'But he was.'

'Unless it was just another accident,' Mum says. We both look at her. 'If nothing else had happened, we wouldn't even be talking like this, would we? We'd just agree it was an awful, terrible accident.'

'Come on, Sarita, you don't believe that. It's not some isolated thing.'

'Nobody saw him in here. All that happened is that you left the radiator draining into the bowl.'

'I know! I know it's my fault! And I'm sorry . . .'

'I'm not talking about fault, I'm just saying—'

'He doesn't work alone,' I say.

'What are you talking about?'

'I gave Christie that water. I pushed Harry . . .'

'We've been through this, Nic,' says Dad. 'You never meant to hurt anyone—'

'—and neither did you. We don't mean to do these things, but somehow we end up doing them. Maybe we're not guilty, but we're not exactly innocent, are we, any of us? We're all part of it.'

They lied to you. It wasn't an accident. It was murder.

'You're not part of this, Nic,' says Dad. 'This was me. I would never, ever have hurt Misty. I love this dog. We all do. Did. And I'm sorry. I'm so, so sorry.'

He sinks to the ground and curls up.

'Stop it. This has got to stop right now.' Mum's got hold of Dad's elbow and she's shaking it. 'Throwing blame around won't help anyone. You've been saying for weeks that these things didn't just happen, Clarke. Well, okay, I believe you now. Okay? Do you hear me? I believe you. And I'm scared. He's in our house. He's found our

201

daughter. Just like you said he would. So now what? What do we do? What the hell do we do?'

Dad's still crying. Mum's shaking him and then she starts to cry, too. I can't remember the last time I saw her cry. She's so self-contained, self-assured. She's the one who keeps calm in a crisis, who others depend on to see their babies safely into the world. She can deal with pain and terror, blood and panic. She can cope with anything at all.

She lets go of Dad and rocks backwards and forwards on her heels.

My mum and dad are in their thirties, but right now they are as helpless and vulnerable as a pair of little kids.

The locket presses coolly against my skin. And I know who to blame, whose fault this really is.

Rob was gone from their lives, left in the past, seventeen years ago. I brought him back. If it wasn't for me, digging around, poking my nose where it shouldn't be, he wouldn't have found us. And because of this, one girl is dead and so many others are in hospital. My jealousy, my pride, my selfishness put them there. I put them there.

And now this. Misty, who I loved more than anything in the world, is dead. Because of me. I wouldn't do what he wanted. I said 'no'. And Misty paid the price.

So it's down to me. I did this, and I've got to put things right.

TWENTY-SEVEN

He starts with a spade and moves on to a pickaxe. Mum and I stand under the sunshade and watch as he swings it above his head, twists his body, brings it over and down, slamming the point into the ground. The earth is solid, unyielding. After ten minutes, he's only scuffed the surface.

He stops and leans on the axe, breathing heavily, staring down.

'This is hopeless,' he says.

'Leave it for now,' Mum says. 'It's still too hot to be pushing yourself like this.'

'I need to soften the ground.'

He strides up the garden and starts unravelling the hose from its coil on the wall.

'But Clarke . . . the water . . .' Mum says.

'I'm not going to get wet and neither is anyone else. I'm just going to let it run on a patch of earth for a minute or two.'

'You can't. There's a hosepipe ban, remember?'

'I've got to do something.'

'I know, but we don't need an appearance in court, do we? Or a fine?'

'Who's going to tell?'

Mum looks significantly back at the row of houses. The lace curtain in the bedroom window next door swings to and fro. Mrs Collins next door isn't the only one who's been watching, but she's the one most likely to ring the council.

'It's not worth the risk,' Mum says.

Dad turns to face the neighbours and spreads his arms out wide. 'My dog's dead! I've got to bury the dog!' he shouts.

The net curtains don't move, but Dad's not looking anyway. Holding the end of the hose he strides down the garden to the patch of slightly disturbed earth.

'Okay, turn it on.'

'No,' Mum says. She folds her arms.

'Turn the bloody thing on!'

Mum holds both hands up and, with a shake of her head, walks back into the kitchen.

'Nic, turn it on, please?' Dad says.

'Really?'

'Just do it. My responsibility. I'll go to bloody prison if I have to.'

I start turning the tap. The metal is warm to the touch.

I twiddle it round and round again. There's a slight juddering in response, but no water.

'Come on, Nic. Keep turning.'

The tap's fully open now, but the hose is limp and empty. 'There's nothing there, Dad.'

He drops the nozzle on to the ground and marches up towards me.

'Dad, I've turned it as much as I can.'

He tries turning it both ways, peers down the garden and then stalks into the kitchen. I follow and find him standing at the kitchen sink, turning the taps there. At the same time a distorted booming sound drifts in through the windows in the front room. I walk to the front door and open it, horribly aware that there will be no dog rushing past my legs to escape this time. Or ever again.

A van is driving slowly along the road with a loud-speaker on its roof.

'Your water has been switched off until further notice. Midlands Water will be installing a standpipe in Mortimer Street within the next hour. We apologise for the inconvenience.'

'What's that?'

'It's off, Dad. They've switched the water off.'

He joins me at the front door and listens to the message as it's repeated.

'That's it, then.' Mum is standing on the stairs behind us. We both turn round. 'It's buckets and plastic bottles from now on.'

'How am I going to dig my hole?'

'I've been thinking, we'd be better off taking her to the

vet's. Have her cremated. We can keep her ashes then, or bury or scatter them. It's better really. I can't stand the thought of something digging her up – there are so many foxes round here. It'll cost, though.'

'Well, I've got the car money. Shall I ring up? Take her now?'

She nods.

'Might as well. It's too hot to keep her here.'

Dad disappears into the lounge and I can hear him on the phone, making arrangements. Mum sits down on the stairs and I join her on the step below.

'I don't want her to go to the vet's,' I say.

'I know, but it's for the best. We'll get her back again soon.'

She starts stroking my hair, like she did when I was little. We sit like this in silence until Dad reappears.

'That's sorted. I've rung for a taxi too.'

'Shall I give you the cash?'

'No, I've got it covered.' Dad squeezes past us and heads upstairs. He pauses on the landing and turns round. 'You know what this means, don't you?' he says.

'What?'

'It means we're safe now. No water. He can't get to us. This house is as safe as it can get.'

He should be right. Logically, he is right. But I'm not convinced.

I can't get the sight of Misty, lying on my bedroom floor, out of my head.

I don't think I'll ever feel safe again.

Dad goes into his bedroom.

'Mum,' I say.

'Yes, love?'

'You and Dad keep saying he's back. Dad's brother. Did you see him before – after he'd died, I mean?'

She sighs. The hand that was stroking my hair stops moving.

'Yes,' she says. 'I saw him in the flood that destroyed my old house. And Dad saw him before that.'

'What happened that time? How did you make him go away?'

'I've been thinking about that. I think it was Dad who did it. He came back into the flooded house looking for me. He was prepared to sacrifice himself in order to save me – he loved me that much. Rob was so full of hate and jealousy. I think it was love that defeated him.'

'Wow.'

She gives a hollow little laugh.

'I know. You wouldn't think to look at us now that we ever loved that hard, that much. But we did. We still do, really. I love your dad and I know he loves me. It's just that life, the business of living, grinds you down. Sometimes you forget what really matters. You forget to tell people how much they mean.'

'I love you, Mum. And I love Dad.'

'I know. And we love you, too. More than anything.'

'Coming down!'

Dad's at the top of the stairs with a blanket bundled up in his arms. It's not just a blanket, though. It's a blanket with something inside.

'The taxi will be here soon.'

'Shall we come with you?' Mum asks.

'They're not particularly nice places, vets' surgeries, are they? Better to say goodbye here. I'll put her in the lounge while we wait.'

He lays the bundle on the sofa and gently opens it up so we can see her one last time. Mum runs her hands over Misty's face and muzzle and gently closes her eyes for her.

'Do you want some time on your own with her, Nic?'

I nod. But once they've left the room, I feel lost. I can't think of anything to say to her except 'sorry'. Over and over again.

I stroke her fur one more time, kiss her forehead and wrap her up in the blanket. The taxi sounds its horn as it draws up outside.

Mum pops her head round the doorway.

'Okay? Or do you need a bit longer?'

I shrug, too teary to speak.

'Oh, love. I'm so sorry. Come here.' She hugs me as Dad picks up the blanket bundle and walks towards the front door.

'I won't be long,' he says. 'You two stay here. I know you'll be safe here, so promise you'll stay put? Okay?'

'We'll be here,' Mum says. 'See you later.' She closes the door behind him. 'You look done in,' she says to me.

'I am,' I say. 'I'd try having a lie down, but I can't face . . .'

'Of course not, stay here. I'll clean your room. It won't take long, then we can both have a nap. Or try to, anyway.'

I perch on the arm of the sofa. I feel numb, hollowed out. Above me I can hear Mum scrubbing my bedroom carpet. When she finishes, she comes downstairs.

'That's better,' she says. 'It doesn't look too bad now. It should be fine when it dries.'

'Thanks,' I say bleakly.

'Come on, Nic. Try having a nap. I'm going to. It's been a long day.'

I follow her upstairs.

'That's it, love,' Mum says. 'A lie down will do us both good.'

I manage half a smile and watch her retreat into her room.

Dad's right. She'll be safe here, until he gets back. It will be one less thing to worry about while I try and work out how to stop Rob.

TWENTY-EIGHT

I heard your dad shouting. You ok?

I don't know what to reply. The feelings I've got right now can't be put into a text.

My phone pings again.

Srsly, Nic, you ok? I'm coming round.

A couple of minutes later and Milton's at the front door. I open up before he can ring the bell – I don't want him waking Mum up.

Seeing him, having to tell him about Misty, is too much. I start crying and it takes a long time to stop. We sit in the front room until the waves of tears calm down and I can speak again.

'So what happened?' Milton asks gently.

'It's all my fault. He warned me and I defied him . . . and he did it.'

'Who? What? You're not making sense.'

He keeps asking me questions until, bit by bit, my story unravels.

'This isn't your fault, Nic. If this is all true, then this guy, ghost, whatever, is evil.'

'It is my fault. I brought him back into our lives. It was this—' I clutch the locket and pull hard, trying to yank it off my neck.

'Whoa, not like that! Here, I'll do it.'

He reaches round the back of my neck and undoes the clasp.

'I hate it. I hate that thing.'

'Have you looked inside?'

I shake my head.

'Do you mind—?'

I shake my head again.

'Hmm, it's really stuck . . .' He's pulling faces as he tries to prise the two halves of the locket apart. 'I need a knife or something.'

'Just leave it. It doesn't matter. The thing's cursed. I'm cursed. I've got to figure a way of sorting everything out.'

'How on earth are you going to do that?'

'I don't know. Mum said that last time Rob was around, love defeated him. My dad was prepared to sacrifice himself to save her.'

'Blimey.'

'I know.' I've got a plan forming in my head, a way to make Rob leave Mum and Dad alone for ever. It's not what I want, but maybe it's what has to happen. 'I made this mess happen, Milton. So I've got to make it go away.

There's got to be . . . sacrifice.'

He looks at me hard, like he's trying to read my mind or something. Then his face changes.

'No, Nic,' he says. 'You mustn't do anything . . . silly.'

'All those girls, Milton. What's one more?'

'I can't believe you're even saying this. You're not thinking straight!' He grips my shoulders and starts to shake me.

'Stop it!' I shout.

'Not until you stop this nonsense! How would losing you possibly help your parents? How would it make anything better? It wouldn't bring any of the girls back. It wouldn't bring Christie back. Or Misty.'

'But maybe it would stop him. If I gave myself, showed him the strength of my love for Mum and Dad . . .'

'No! No way! I won't let you!'

'For Christ's sake, Milton, you're not my dad or something. You can't stop me!'

'I can. I'm a lot bigger than you!'

He wraps his arms round me now, holds me in a sort of bear hug.

'But I'm stronger!' I'm trying to wrestle him off me, but he's holding firm. After a little while my body starts to shake. I'm laughing, at how silly it is to be tussling like children. And then I'm crying, because none of this is funny. I'm not a child any more. I've got to stand up and be counted. I don't want to, but I know it's what I've got to do. And it doesn't matter if Milton tries to stop me or Dad does, one way or another I'll find a way to break free, and I'll do what I have to do.

Milton rests his chin on the top of my head and rocks me gently.

'I won't let you go,' he says.

'You can't hold on for ever.'

But, secretly, I wish he would.

We're quiet for a while, leaning against each other, holding on. We're both sweaty and sticky, but it doesn't matter. What matters is being held, feeling safe, just for a moment.

I close my eyes, and a picture of Sammi Shah comes into my head. The girl in the reservoir. I get a choking feeling gripping my throat. *On your own. Water all around you. The rising panic. No one coming to help.*

I don't know if I can do it, even if it would save Mum and Dad. I don't know if I'm brave enough. I don't know how strong my love is.

'Maybe I can reason with him,' I say, hearing myself backtracking and hating myself for it. 'I'll find him and talk with him.'

'Where is he?'

Milton releases me from his hug a little, so we can look at each other.

'He's always in water,' I say. 'Ours has been turned off, so I can't just pop into the shower. The obvious place is the swimming pool.'

'It's closed, Nic. They made the announcement halfway through the afternoon. "Closed with immediate effect".'

'Not the pool, then. Umm, somewhere with water . . . it'll have to be . . . it'll have to be Turley Res.'

'You're kidding.'

'It's only a bus ride away. And I know — well, I think — he's been there before, because of . . . you know . . . that girl. I'll wear the locket.'

'Nic. Really. You know how dangerous it is there. You know what happened . . .'

'I won't go right in. Just enough to talk to him.'

'Seriously, Nic? No.'

'I'm going to do it, Milton.'

There must be something about the tone of my voice, because he breathes a long sigh out and then says, 'Not on your own, you're not. I'm coming with you.'

'Will you?'

''Course. When are we going?'

'Now. While Mum's asleep. Before Dad gets back.'

He sighs again.

'This is madness, but give me five minutes. So I can nip home and fetch my wallet?'

'Okay. Outside mine in five. And Milton . . .'

'Yeah?'

'Thanks.'

TWENTY-NINE

Milton stares at the sign tacked on to the chain-link fence next to the padlocked gate.

DANGER. DEEP WATER. NO SWIMMING. NO PADDLING. KEEP OUT. By order of the Midlands Water Co.

'They're trying to tell us something, Nic. Let's go home.'

'You didn't think we were going in by the gate, did you?'

'What—?'

'Come on.'

I take hold of his hand and dive through some bushes, following the line of the fence. The undergrowth is scrubby and scratchy against my legs. Behind me, Milton keeps making funny noises, high-pitched squeaks.

'What's wrong?'

'These branches. You keep pinging them into me!'

'Sorry!'

I let go of his hand so that I can hold the low branches back for him, and we tread more slowly until we reach a spot that looks promising. There's a sturdy fencepost, and the top of the wire next to it has been pulled down a little where others have climbed over.

'This looks good. Can you give me a leg up?'

'Nic—'

'Come on, Milton, this is obviously where everyone gets in.' I'm sounding a lot braver than I feel, but I feel like I've got to, since Milton's feet are cold enough for both of us.

'Okay.' He cups his hands near the fencepost and I step up and give a little spring, trusting my weight to him and reaching for the top of the post. He grunts. I feel my foot sinking a little, and then he recovers himself and boosts me up.

'Have you got it? Are you there?'

My other foot finds a toehold where one of the metal links has broken. I transfer some of my weight on to it and, when it holds, brace myself and then push from that foot. I haul with both arms and suddenly I'm up, teetering perilously on the top of the post.

'God, now what?' I say. But there's nothing else to do but jump. I land heavily, grazing my knees, then stand up and brush away the worst of the dust and grit with my hands.

'That wasn't too bad,' I say through the fence to Milton. 'You next.'

He puffs out his cheeks.

'Unless you want to just wait here. I won't be long . . .'

He must have caught the uncertainty in my voice, because without saying anything, he breathes heavily a couple of times, then launches himself at the fence. It's not pretty, but less than ten seconds later he's standing next to me in a cloud of dust. We both turn to look at the reservoir.

It's a huge flat expanse of water, obviously smaller than it usually is, because it's bounded by a wide, gently sloping orange-yellow 'beach'. Beyond that there's a scrubby strip of dried-up grass most of the way round, with a concrete bank at one end.

A heat haze is shimmering above the water. There's no noise apart from the background murmur of traffic. It's a peaceful place. Hard to imagine that this is where Sammi died.

'Right.' I quickly strip down to my swimming costume, handing my clothes to Milton to hold. He looks at me, blinking rapidly, pressing his dry lips together.

'What is it?' I ask.

'I can't swim,' he says.

'I'm not expecting you to come in with me.'

'No, I know, it's just that . . . if you needed me . . . if something went wrong . . . I'm not sure I'd be much use.'

'You've got your phone, haven't you?'

'Yeah.'

'We're sorted, then. If anything happens, ring for help. Not that anything will happen. Everything's going to be fine.' I try to keep my tone matter-of-fact, businesslike. 'I'll be back in a minute.'

I march away from him, across the dry grass, and then slow down as I reach the gravelly beach.

'Nic!' Milton shouts.

I look over my shoulder.

'You need this, don't you?'

The locket dangles from his hand, catching the light as it turns. I retrace my steps, and he puts the chain round my neck and does up the clasp.

I set off again. I keep my pace steady this time, not allowing any hesitation, even when I reach the water. I wade into the warm shallows, watching and listening all the time. Further in, the water creeps up my legs, over my bum, up to my middle. I turn round. Milton's come forward so he's at the water's edge.

'Anything?' he shouts to me.

'Nothing.'

'That's far enough. He's obviously not here. Let's go home now.'

The water is crystal clear. The only movement on the surface caused by me.

'No, not yet.'

Where are you, Rob? Maybe it's because Milton's here. Rob always disappeared in the pool when there were other people about. But I could still hear him, sense him. I've got nothing now. No hint of his presence. No whispers in my ear. I'm going to have to go deeper. I wade a little further until the water is up to my armpits.

'Nic! Really, come back now.'

I ignore Milton, take a breath and bob down where I

stand, so that the water closes over me. I forgot to bring my goggles, but I don't need them. I keep my eyes open and look around. The underwater landscape is featureless. Gravelly silt beneath my feet, stretching as far as I can see in all directions. Clear water above. Sun breaking through the surface, illuminating what's below. The blocked-up, blocked-in noise of water in my ears. That sense of pressure.

It may be featureless, but it's beautiful too. I've got the urge to swim. I lean forward, kick my feet up and gently move through the water. My body uses all the moves it's learnt from years of training, but everything feels different here. The resistance of the water against my limbs, the sense of weight and weightlessness and space. Still keeping under, I weave around, my hair splaying out around my face. I've lost track of time. I've forgotten why I came here. I've forgotten the trauma and loss. I'm caught up in the moment, the ecstasy of swimming free.

When I surface and look around, I'm a long way from Milton. I can't see his features any more, but I can see that he's waded out into the water, up to his waist. Even at this distance I can sense his panic.

'Nic!' he hollers. 'Nic! Over here!'

He's a big lad, standing solidly in the water, but I remember the look on his face when he told me he couldn't swim, and now, seeing him surrounded by water, he looks desperately vulnerable.

What if Rob's here, after all? What if he's heading for Milton, not me?

No, no. Not Milton. I can't bear it.

'Get out of the water! Get out, Milton!'

I start swimming towards him as fast as I can. He isn't moving. God, why isn't he moving?

I reach him and stand up, smoothing my hair back from my face.

'Milton, what are you doing in here? For God's sake, get out!'

He seems to wobble where he stands, windmilling his arms to get his balance. He's going to go in. I put my arm round his waist, try to steady him. He's breathing hard, puffing and panting through pursed lips.

'Milton, it's all right. We're going to walk back now.'

We turn in the water and slowly wade back to the shore. He sits on the beach, trying to get his breath back.

'What on earth were you doing? You told me you couldn't swim!'

'You were gone for ages. I thought . . . I thought that . . . oh, God. I couldn't reach you. I couldn't come any further. I thought I was going to slip and the water was too deep and . . .'

I put my wet hand on his arm.

'I was just swimming. I'm sorry. I didn't think. I'm really sorry.'

He shakes his head. 'It's okay. Did you see him?' he asks.

'No. Nothing. Nothing at all. Did you? Is that why you were losing your footing?'

He wipes his face with his hand.

'No. I just panicked, that's all. I've never been good round water.'

'Jesus, Milton.'

I brought a little towel with me, but I don't need it in the heat. I just squeeze my hands along my arms and legs to get most of the water off, and the rest dries in a minute or two. I hand the towel to Milton and he dries his arms and legs. Then he gets to his feet and we stand looking at the water.

'If he's not here, where is he?' I say.

Milton shrugs.

'I dunno. Let's get out of here before someone sees us. Are you putting these back on?' He picks up my clothes and holds them out to me. I slip my T-shirt and shorts over my half-dry costume and we walk back to the fence. Milton helps me over, and then takes a couple of attempts to get over himself.

We trail back to the bus stop. The timetable shows we've just missed the bus. There isn't another one for nearly an hour, so we start walking. Heat radiates up from the pavement and the cool flush from the reservoir water is soon forgotten by my sweaty skin. My legs feel achy and tired. It's going to be a long walk home.

'Milton?'

'Yeah.'

'Rob told me before that we were playing a game. Hide-and-seek.'

'O-kay.'

'So I think he's hiding somewhere, and I've got to find him. I've got to use all the clues he's given me. And I've got to take Mum and Dad to him.'

'I thought you didn't want to.'

'I don't. I'm not going to. But I will find him.'

'Where else can you look? Like you said, we're running out of water round here.'

'I don't know. I need to think about everything he's ever said to me, everything that's happened over the past week.'

'Maybe he's just gone, Nic. It's worth just waiting, see if this might just be over. The water supply is pretty much drying up around here. Maybe he's gone with it.'

'I wish that was true. But Misty died today. He was there today, Milton. In my house. Killing my best friend. No offence.'

'None taken. I still think you should wait a while, though. Think it through some more. You've had a rough day, a rough couple of weeks. Don't rush into anything.'

'Maybe.'

Milton stops walking. I plod further on, worried that if I stop I'll never start again. The heat and the stress are really taking their toll now. Instead, I turn round and walk slowly backwards, facing him.

'Promise me you won't do anything on your own,' Milton says. 'I'm your wing man, remember? Cross your heart or something. Show me you mean it.'

'I promise,' I say, feebly tracing a cross in the air in front of me, and Milton catches me up and takes my hand in his.

But as I lie in bed later, too hot to sleep, I'm unbearably aware of the dark patch on the carpet next to my bed where Mum has cleaned and cleaned again. I'll never be able to sleep in this room unless I get rid of the evil that killed Misty. I'll never be truly safe, and neither will Mum or Dad. I'll be haunted in the same way that they have been – always vigilant, always fearful of him coming back. And I don't think he's finished with us. Not yet.

So where is he? What has he been trying to tell me?

Bring them back to me.

I thought he meant bring Mum and Dad into the water, but maybe it's something else. Where did this all start? Where could they be brought 'back' to?

Kingsleigh. Of course.

Years ago, even before I was born, it all started with Mum, Dad and his brother, Rob. The lake in the park.

I open my laptop and scroll back to Milton's message with all the links to the reports and start working my way through. And near the end of one article, there's this:

Kerry Adams, 34, Robert's mother, was too distraught to comment at the time this went to press.

Kerry Adams.

K.A.

I've seen those initials somewhere before.

I slip off the bed and fish the envelope containing the locket out of my shorts pocket. It's a bit battered now from being carried about, but the writing is still clear, and I study it now.

Found with Nicola. 22/1/17. K.A.

Kerry Adams. Rob and Dad's mum – my grandma. Someone else my dad has never talked about. His own mother . . . someone I don't remember ever meeting. I don't even know if she's alive.

223

I do the sums on my fingers. She should be fifty-one now, no age at all for a granny.

I try googling her name. Not many hits, a couple of lines in the Kingsleigh local press: two appearances at magistrates' court. Name, address, offence. One for shoplifting. One just last month for being drunk in a public place. So she's still there.

I think of Grandpa – his orderly life, the careful, almost fussy way he kept his house and garden, his regimented daily routine. Kerry sounds like a different sort of person altogether. Is that why Dad kept me away from her?

Whatever the reason, she was in Kingsleigh seventeen years ago when she lost a son. She was there in 2017, too. She 'found' me – and, with me, the locket that brought Rob into my life.

Everything's pointing the same way. So now I know what I've got to do next. And it's something I've got to do on my own.

I can't tell Mum and Dad, because if I take them to him then I'm certain in my bones that they are in mortal danger. And I can't take Milton, because this afternoon's escapade at the reservoir showed me how vulnerable he is around water. I can't lose him. I can't lose any of them.

This is my mess, and I've got to follow my hunch and go to Kingsleigh before anyone else gets hurt.

THIRTY

I creep downstairs in the soft light of dawn, surprised not to see Misty at the bottom of the stairs, looking up expectantly, lead held in her soft mouth. Then I remember. She'll never be there again.

Choking back tears, I open the front door, slip out and close it behind me as quietly as I can. The first coach to Bristol is in twenty minutes. I should make it if I run.

I've only got a couple of minutes to get my ticket from the booth and find the bus. There are two women in front of me in the queue, both sixty-something with oversized suitcases. I stand behind them, gasping, chest heaving, wiping my face with my T-shirt while they discuss which type of ticket will suit them best. Eventually they settle on a couple of open return tickets, and only then does one of the old biddies get her purse out and start to look for a card to pay with. Then she takes an age putting the card back in her purse, the purse back in her bag, and her bag back across her body, before they finally start trundling their cases out of the way.

'Ticket to Bristol,' I blurt out, stepping past one of the cases.

'Single or return?'

'I don't care!'

The woman behind the desk looks at me steadily, clearly not going to do anything until I give her a sensible answer.

'Return, please.'

I slide the cash across the counter, grab my ticket and run, looking at the destination signs above each bay. Newcastle. Liverpool. Manchester. Cardiff. Bristol! I swing round the metal barrier just as the pneumatic doors of the coach hiss shut.

I look up at the driver. He smiles, shrugs and puts the coach into reverse. It starts to roll slowly backwards. No! I dart forward and slap my hands against the door. The driver slams on the brakes and shakes his head at me.

Behind me, someone shouts. 'Oi! You! Step behind the barriers!'

I look round. A guy in a high-vis jacket is heading my way.

I turn back to the driver, clasp my hands in prayer and mouth the word 'Please' at him. He shakes his head again – but then, to my amazement, there's another hiss and the doors shudder open.

'Oh my God, thank you. Thank you.'

I scramble aboard. Behind me, there's another shout.

'That's me in trouble now,' the driver says. 'Against the rules to stop like that.'

'Sorry,' I say.

'My call. That prick gets right on my nerves.' He looks towards the high-vis guy, who's now standing open-mouthed. 'Find a seat quickly. We're off now.'

'Okay, thanks. Like, *really*, thanks.'

I lurch along the aisle as the coach pulls out of the bus station. I can only find one spare seat. It's by the window, and the woman in the next seat has spread her things all over it.

''Scuse me,' I say. 'Can I sit here, please?'

She looks at me, and there's a pause before she sighs and starts moving her things: a handbag, a plastic lunch-box, a thermos, a couple of books and a magazine. She clutches it all to her stomach and huffs out of the seat, doubled over.

'Thank you.' I sit down and take out my phone, earphones and water, then squeeze my rucksack into the space by my legs while she settles back into her seat. The coach swings out on to the main road and I'm pressed against the window as my neighbour slides across the seat. She's twice my size and age, wearing shorts and a vest top like me. The amount of flesh pressing against me makes me squirm inside, but there's nothing I can do until we've stopped going round this corner.

I'm suddenly aware that, despite the unwelcome close-ness of my neighbour, I'm actually on my own. I've never travelled alone – hardly been anywhere at all – and now I'm speeding away from the only people I've ever known, heading towards a place I haven't been to since I was tiny. A place I don't really know. A place which, if I let myself think about it, terrifies me.

My mind's racing. My body's on red alert. What on earth am I doing? I'm out of my depth.

I try to remember why I'm here, and my thoughts head back to Misty. I loved her, love her still, and Rob killed her. He'll keep killing unless someone can stop him, and that someone has to be me. Worrying isn't going to help. I need to focus on what I'm going to do when I get to Kingsleigh. I need a plan.

I could go straight to the lake. 'Back' to where Rob drowned. As hot as I am, I get goosebumps thinking about it. If he's there, he's not going to be happy that I haven't brought Mum and Dad with me. He's going to be really, really angry. Will he kill me instead? Would that be enough to bring all this to an end or would he still go after them?

Who would miss me if I died? The girls on the team wouldn't care – if they even survive the legionella, that is. Harry couldn't care less. There's Milton, I suppose, but mostly it's Mum and Dad. It would destroy them. But maybe they'd grow to be proud of me, if they realised I'd done this for them . . . and perhaps I'll see Misty again. Misty . . . I'm welling up again now. I can't spend the journey crying. Come on, Nic, concentrate.

If I'm going to die, then maybe I should try and find my grandmother first. I'd like to know the whole truth, understand how the story started. Yes, that's what I'm going to do. I have my plan now, so I try to zone out, calm the butterflies that are fighting in my stomach.

We've just hit the motorway when my companion opens her plastic sandwich box, releasing the unmistakeable smell of boiled egg. I put my hand across my mouth and turn my face to the window. It's stifling in here and the smell makes me gag. I reach up, tug at the air blower and twiddle it round – nothing. It's not working. God, this is going to be a long journey.

I undo the top of my water bottle and start sipping to help calm my stomach. I gaze out of the window, watching the blur of flat, yellow fields, blitzed to nearly nothing by the summer's heat. The sun's shining directly at me. I'm sweating, starting to feel a little dizzy.

I drink more water. Soon the first bottle's empty and I wiggle my bag round until I can get the empty bottle in and fish out the second one. I hear my dad's voice: 'Just sip it. Take it easy.' Even though he's not with me, he's still in my head. All his rules and regulations have been drummed into me. Even so, I unscrew the lid and drink. Then I tip a very little into my hand and rub it on to my face, forehead and neck, desperate to try anything that might cool me down.

And there it is.

Rob's voice.

On your own. That's not good. I warned you.

And the butterflies are back. Except it's not butterflies, it's something bigger, with claws – gripping, twisting, tearing at my insides . . .

I can't bring them to you. I can't do it. I'm right, though, aren't I? You wanted me to come to Kingsleigh?

I wanted you to bring them, you little bitch.

I bring the hem of my vest top up and wipe my face. Wipe him away.

Oh God, what have I got myself into?

My neighbour's finished her sandwiches, but the smell remains. She's breaking into a bag of cheese and onion crisps now, stuffing handfuls in, chewing with her mouth open.

Maybe some music will help chase Rob's voice out of my head. I wake my phone up and start scrolling through my tracks, but my attention's caught by the text icon. Ten new messages. Ten? I open up my inbox. Messages from Dad, Mum and Milton.

Mum and Dad's messages are anxious:

Where are you?

Nic, ring home.

I can't tell them. I can't risk them finding out where I am, where I'm heading. I know I'm in danger, but so are they, and maybe I can keep them safe.

I'm suddenly aware of the water sloshing about inside me. I've drunk more than a litre in less than half an hour. Oh God. I need the loo.

''Scuse me.' I grab my bag and try to stand up, crouching under the overhang of the lockers above. My neighbour looks at me with undisguised irritation and doesn't move.

''Scuse me. I just need to—'

Finally, with a lot of oniony puffing, she starts gathering her things together again and eases herself out of her seat. I squeeze past and head for the toilet. The 'engaged' sign is on, so I lurk in the aisle, trying not to fall into anyone's lap. People are already looking worn down by the stuffy heat. Glazed eyes, hands flopping over the armrests.

The toilet door opens. The guy coming out won't meet my eyes.

'Sorry,' he mumbles, as he goes past. 'It's not . . . there's a bit of a . . .'

The smell hits the back of my throat even before I push the door open. There's paper sticking to the inside of the bowl, a nest of it at the bottom which doesn't manage to hide the mess. I jerk back, letting the door slam shut.

I've got to get off this coach. I can't do two more hours on here. I stagger to the front. The driver eyes me warily in his mirror.

'You need to stop the bus,' I say. 'I need to get off.'

He shakes his head. 'I did you a favour letting you on. Stay put, love. We'll be at the services soon.'

'You don't understand, I need to get off. I need to use the toilet but it's blocked.'

'Only ten minutes 'til we reach the services.'

'I feel sick.'

He turns his head quickly and checks me out. 'Use a bag. There are bags in the nets on the back of the seats.'

'I'm not using a bag. I need some fresh air. I want to get off!'

Everyone's looking now, but I don't care.

'We're on the motorway, love,' a pensioner in a vest says, leaning out of his seat and tapping me on the arm. 'Sit down, there's a good girl, and stop making a fuss.'

'We won't stop 'til the services,' someone else chimes in. 'You might as well sit down.'

There's a chorus of them now.

'You're making us all feel hotter.'

'Yeah, sit down!'

I'm not going to win. I make my way down the bus again and wait while the egg-and-cheese-woman gathers all her things once more, stands up and lets me in. I squash myself into the corner, turning my face away from her and look out of the window. Perhaps by being very still I can stop the feeling of the water swilling around inside me.

I don't see the blur of fields and farms. I don't really see my reflection. I can only see the nightmarish parade of images in my head . . . Christie's face as she started to choke. The pattern Harry's blood made as it fanned out in the water. Misty's lifeless eyes and the dark wet patch around her head. And a boy, lying on the bottom of a swimming pool – pale skin, marked and grazed.

I close my eyes and try to picture myself somewhere else, anywhere else but this metal sweat-box on wheels. And I'm back at the pool. The perfect turquoise rectangle. It was my place for a while. The place where I felt happiest. Now it's been drained. A turquoise hole in the ground. Everything's changed. Ruined. Spoilt.

Something's digging into the top of my leg. I fish in my pocket and bring out the locket. What was it Milton said?

'If you open it there might be clues in there . . .'

The metal is cool in my hand. My sweaty fingers keep slipping as I try to prise it open. My thumbnail tears and a little bead of blood appears at the corner. What else can I use? I try inserting the side of the zip pull on my bag into the groove at the edge of the locket. My companion gives me a sideways glance, then pointedly goes back to her sudoku.

I twist the zip pull and it slips, but the next time something gives, just a little. I try again and the catch opens, reluctantly. I let go of the zipper and force the sides open, like the covers of a miniature book. Inside is dry as a bone. There are two photos, each behind a little window in either half of the locket. Two faces looking out at me. I've seen one of the photos before. A boy in school uniform, sneering at the camera. Rob.

The other side is a girl, a close-up of her face. She's pouting for the camera. I can just see part of a silver chain around her neck, the top of a naked shoulder. It's Mum.

Mum and Rob.

Not Mum and Dad.

'You wouldn't think to look at us now that we ever loved that hard, that much.'

But who did she love? Which brother?

I stare at the two photos until they're imprinted in my brain. Mum and Rob. Rob and Mum. So many secrets. So many lies . . .

'We're stopping. If you want some air, now's your chance.'

Someone's hand is on my shoulder, shaking me. I jerk my eyes open: I must have been asleep. I look out of the window; we're inching through a car park, swinging into a diagonal parking space alongside other coaches. My mouth is open and I can feel the tickling of drool at the corner and down the side of my chin. I put my hand up to wipe it away, and the open locket falls into my lap. And there are their faces again – Mum and Rob. I snap the locket shut and stuff it back into my pocket.

There's a horrible taste in my mouth – metallic and raw. I try to swallow but all the moisture has dribbled out of me. My throat is dry and scrapey. I reach down beside me for my water bottle, but it's empty now, rolling on the floor between my feet.

'Are you getting off?' It's Miss Egg-and-Cheese. 'You made enough fuss earlier. We're here now.'

She joins the queue of people shuffling slowly towards the front. I take a moment to come round a bit more, appreciating the welcome gap next to me, the absence of flesh pressing against my own. I let the others file past me and then join the end of the line.

I head over to the service station. Inside, the air conditioning is working and it's like stepping into another world. Blissful, cool, clean. I dash to the ladies', then head for the chilled cabinet in the store to stock up with water, pick up some mints to freshen my mouth.

Next to the till my eyes run over the headlines of the newspapers in the rack. They stop at one: LEGIONELLA SUSPECTED AS SWIM TEAM STRUCK DOWN. I pick up the paper.

Council officials confirmed that they are investigating a suspected outbreak of legionnaires' disease at Narrowbridge Swimming Pool, after several members of a girls' swimming team fell ill. The council has confirmed that the pool will be closed until investigations have been completed, and will also undergo a thorough industrial clean as an additional precaution. In an official statement released earlier today, the council stressed that 'the health and safety of our customers is our first priority.'

A spokesman from South Birmingham General Hospital said that in total seven girls had been admitted, two of whom were in intensive care. A further statement is due to be issued later tonight.

The air conditioning is blowing straight down from the vent above me, and I'm shivering violently. Two in intensive care. How many of the girls will end up on Dad's spreadsheet? And will I be the last entry?

'You buying that?' The girl on the till is looking at the paper in my hands.

'Yes. No.' I put the paper back. 'Just the water, and these, thanks.'

I pay, put my things in my bag, then head back to the coach. The heat outside is intense – it's shimmering off the tarmac. I clamber back on to the coach. The air's no cooler, but it's a little fresher after a quarter of an hour with the door open.

I check my phone again. More messages coming in all the time. I put it into silent mode.

The sun's climbing higher in the sky as we draw into Bristol. At the coach station I ask for the bus to Kingsleigh and get straight on it.

THIRTY-ONE

It's not easy to find Kerry Adams. I managed to get a post-code for the address from the court reports and I plug it into the direction finder on my phone, but when I get there, the tiny terraced house is boarded up. I knock on the door even so, and eventually there's a shout from down the road. A young woman, with a fag trailing out of her mouth, is peering out of her front door.

'Give it a rest. She's not there. Went away a month ago.'

'Do you know where she went?'

'One of the flats on Hunter Street.'

'Have you got the number?'

'Nah. Sorry.'

The door closes again. I find Hunter Street on the map and set off again. When I get there, I ask for help in a run-down corner shop that seems to sell any type of booze a person could want. The man behind the till knows her. He sends me to number 11, a ground floor flat in an unappetising block.

I ring the doorbell.

'Can't you read? I don't buy door-to-door. I've got a sign up.'

The woman who squints through the gap is only small, her eyes just above the level of the chain that's pulled taut, keeping me out.

'I'm not selling anything,' I say. 'I've come to see you. If you're Kerry Adams, that is.'

The eyes narrow.

'Who wants her?'

'Me! I'm her granddaughter. My name's Nic. Nicola Adams. My dad's Carl – calls himself Clarke these days.'

The door shuts. For a moment I'm wondering whether I should start knocking again or give up and go away, then I hear the rattle of the chain and the door swings open. The woman stands in full view, looking me up and down. I guess I'm doing the same to her. She's tiny. Her hair is thin and ratty, just below shoulder length. She's wearing a crumpled sundress with shoelace straps. There's nothing on her feet.

Our eyes meet, and now there's the recognition I was hoping for. Her eyes are Rob's eyes, Dad's eyes. There's no mistaking the likeness.

'Nicola,' she says. 'Little Nicola.'

'Not so little,' I say.

'You were when I last saw you. You were this high.' She holds her hand out in front of her, indicating the height of a tot, then peers past me. 'Is Carl with you?' I shake my head. 'No? What are you doing here? You should have told me you were coming. I would've . . . well, I would've . . . oh, you'd better come in.'

She stands aside and I walk into the hallway. There are four doors leading off it.

'Go through to the kitchen. Second door on the right, that's it.'

The kitchen is a mess. The worktops are littered with empty packets and cans, cups used as ashtrays. The sink has a layer of cans floating in scummy grey water. There's an empty food bowl on the floor, next to a full water bowl, both sitting on a rectangle of newspaper that's scuffed up at the corners and dotted with old food. She sees me looking.

'They're Ella's. Seem to have got myself a cat. She's out somewhere. Do you want a drink?'

'Um, no thanks.' I'd rather die of thirst than drink anything from this kitchen.

'Well, I could do with one. Settle me nerves a bit. Having you turn up out of the blue, it's a shock. A good sort of one, don't get me wrong. Still a shock, though. There's some cans in the fridge.'

I take the hint and open the fridge door. There's an open tin of cat food in one of the door pockets, and rows and rows of lager cans. That's all. I pass her a can.

'Go on,' Kerry says, 'help yourself.'

'Um, no thanks. I don't really . . . I haven't . . . it's okay.'

'I haven't drunk tap water for years, and now they're saying it's not safe anyway. Just goes to show, doesn't it?'

'Um, yes, I suppose . . .'

Would it be rude to make my excuses and leave now? I know the answer, so I let her lead me into the lounge. It's a bit cleaner in here. A few cans lying on the floor, some heaps of free newspapers. There are hardly any decorations or personal touches, though. Just a couple of saggy couches, an ancient electric fire and some photos on the mantelpiece, one of them the old school one that I've already seen. Her two boys in their school uniform.

She sits on one sofa, I sit on the other, at the end nearest to her.

'Your mum and dad know where you are?'

I shake my head.

'Like that, is it? That's how my boys were. I never knew where they were from one day to the next. That was one of my mistakes. I should've known. If I'd made them tell me every time they went out, then maybe they wouldn't have got into so much trouble. Maybe Rob wouldn't have . . . maybe he'd still be . . . '

'I'm not like that,' I say quickly. 'Not normally. Dad keeps tabs on me. He always knows where I am.'

'Ah, that's good. He's better at this than I ever was, then. Is that him?' She can hear my phone buzzing in my bag.

'Probably.'

'Get it out, then. Tell him you're here. Your poor mum and dad must be going spare.'

'I . . . I don't want to. I want a bit of . . . a bit of space.'

'Just tell him you're safe, then. You can do that at least, can't you?'

'Yeah, I s'pose.'

There are thirty new messages now, from Mum, Dad and Milton. And now I realise how selfish I've been. Kerry – Nan – is right. Mum and Dad are probably going out of their minds with worry. And Milton's been a true friend.

I've been wrong to leave them all hanging.

So I send them each a quick text while Kerry watches and swigs from her can – I'm okay. Safe and sound. Taking some time out. See you soon. That sort of thing.

Of course, my phone goes even crazier then, but I put it back in my bag.

'That's better,' Kerry says. 'Save them worrying.'

She takes another long drink, watching me all the time. I feel like I'm being put on the spot, like it's up to me to make all the running.

'It's very . . . nice . . . here,' I say.

'It'll do. It's a lot nicer than the flat I had when the boys were at home. Got condemned in the end. Damp right through, and mould, something terrible. Not fit for human habitation, that's what they said.'

'So this isn't like where Dad grew up?'

'No, love. It was a dump – and, to be honest, I didn't help. Didn't keep it nice. Wasn't a very good . . . never have been . . . ' She clears her throat. 'When I got this place I tried to, you know, turn over a new leaf. Clean. Tidy. Respectable.'

Oh, God. I can't imagine what her previous places were like if this is clean and tidy. I don't say anything, but maybe my face has given my feelings away. She leans forward, resting her forearms on her thighs.

'I do my best, Nicola. My doctor used to call me a functioning alcoholic, see.' Again, I can't think of anything to say. I'm picturing the two little boys in the photograph, left in the care of this shambolic woman in a flat that got condemned. 'Functioning alcoholic, yeah, but to be honest, I'm not functioning all that well these days.' She starts laughing to herself, but soon stops. 'It's not funny, is it? Not really.'

It's impossible to talk to her. I can't find the right words. I can't find any words. She's so different to anyone I know. But she's my gran.

'You never said what you're doing here,' she reminds me. 'Why would you come all this way to see me?'

'I found out about . . . Uncle Rob . . . and about Mum and Dad changing their names, and I wanted to find out more. You said I was this high when you last saw me,' I say, holding my hand out level in front of me. 'So when was that? Why did we stop seeing each other?'

She takes another swig from the can.

'You were only three or thereabouts. You moved away, that's when it all stopped. Your mum and dad went up to Birmingham, changed their names and all.'

'My dad said they wanted to make a fresh start.'

'He wanted to get away from here. This place. Me, maybe.'

'Why, though?'

'I nearly lost you, Nicola. That's what drove them away.'

'You nearly lost me . . . when I was three, in 2017?' I remember the words on the envelope.

'Yeah, that's right. It would have been 2017. January.'

241

'You nearly lost me, but you found me again – and you found this with me?'

I reach into my pocket and bring out the locket.

She gasps, leans further forward and takes the silver pendant in her palm.

'Yes,' she says. 'God, this necklace . . .'

'Where? Where did you find me?'

She looks up at me, her eyes threaded with sore-looking red veins.

'Can you tell me about it? Please.'

She sniffs and sits back down on her sofa. She's cradling her can, turning it round and round. Her mouth is working, but she's not saying anything.

'Please, I need to know.'

I tuck my legs up underneath me and lean on the arm of the sofa. Kerry responds, leaning back a little and turning towards me.

'It was just after Christmas. Your mum was at the hospital, just finishing her training, and your dad was doing a shift at the factory site, demolishing it. They asked me to look after you. I was sober then, had been for a while. It was a beautiful day, very cold but clear. I wrapped you up properly, made sure you'd be warm enough, and we walked to the park. You loved it, running around, playing in the snow. We got to the lake and it was frozen right over.'

'The lake? The same lake as . . .?'

She nods.

'I like to go there. It helps me to think about him. My boy. He was only seventeen. I miss him, you know.'

'Of course.'

'Anyway, it was getting close to dinnertime and I thought, I'll just have a smoke and a little rest and then we'll head back up to the High Street, share a bag of chips. I must have only taken my eyes off you for a minute. I looked around and you weren't there. And then I saw you, out on the ice, and you turned to wave and then you . . . disappeared. Went right through. And I couldn't do anything, couldn't move. I just stood there, watching the place where you'd been. Other people weren't so . . . they rescued you, went out on to the ice. One man got in the water and got you out. They brought you back to me. You looked like a little doll, a frozen little doll, but you were alive. I held you, close, and rocked you backwards and forwards. Backwards and forwards.'

'And the locket?' How do I know what she's going to say before she says it?

'The chain was all wrapped around your fingers.'

'That's so weird.'

'Yes. Especially as I'd seen it before. Seen your mum wearing it.'

The photo in the locket. The glimpse of chain round Mum's neck. So this is this the same one? It must be.

'So how come I had it? How could that possibly happen?'

She shrugs.

'I don't know, darlin'. Sometimes I think it was a gift. My boy gave it to you. He saved you and he was trying to let me know what he'd done. Sometimes I wonder if . . .'

'If what?'

243

Her voice is very quiet now, hardly more than a whisper. ' . . . if he wanted to keep you there.'

Saved me . . . or pulled me under. His voice. *Got you.* Thirteen years and now I'm nearly back where it started. The lake. He *has* to be at the lake.

I shiver, try to focus on Kerry.

'What was he like? Rob?'

'People said all kinds of things about him, and he wasn't no angel. I'm not daft, I know he did things he shouldn't have done. But nobody knows a boy like his mother does. And I know he was a good boy deep down. It's just that people hardly ever saw that. Saw what I saw.'

He was a good boy. Maybe he was once. But he's killed and killed again since then. He'll keep killing unless I stop him.

'If you could see him again, see him now, what would you say to him?'

She sighs, and puts her can down on the floor next to her.

'I talk to him all the time, love. I go to the lake and I can see him, like he used to be. My little boy.'

'You see him?'

She nods, reaches for her packet of cigarettes and takes one out. It trembles between her fingers, unlit.

'He's never gone away. Not for me. He's still here, with me. He always will be.'

I watch as she manages to light the fag and draws the smoke deep into her lungs. She turns her head to blow the smoke away from me.

'I see him, too,' I say.

She looks back at me, mouth open. The cigarette falls from her fingers on to the carpet.

'Kerry! Nan! Look out!'

She keeps staring, oblivious. I dart forward and pick up the cigarette. The carpet is smouldering. I stamp on it, grind my foot round on the spot.

'I think that's got it,' I say. I'm still holding the fag. I put it in the nearest ashtray and sit down again. Kerry's still frozen, like she's in some sort of trance. I reach over and touch her hand.

'Kerry? Nan?'

She looks down at her hand and mine, then back up at me.

'You see him,' she murmurs. 'Rob. My Rob. So he's not dead . . .'

I stroke the back of her hand with my thumb.

'He is dead, Kerry. It's just . . . he's just . . . a sort of ghost, I think.'

'What are you saying?'

'I can see him sometimes, talk to him. But he comes and goes. He lives through water. The thing is—' How can I say this? How can tell her Rob's a serial killer? 'The thing is, he's not happy. He's . . . restless.'

She gives a sob and her free hand goes up to her mouth.

'My boy!'

I don't know if I can carry on, but I must.

'He's . . . he's been hurting people. Girls.'

She wrenches her other hand from under mine.

'You're just like the others,' she says, her eyes narrow

and hard. 'Spreading lies about my boy. Telling tales.'

'No! I don't want it to be like this. I didn't want any of this. But it's real. It's happening.'

'What is? What's going on?'

'He's . . . he's killed a lot of girls. Drowned them. He's dangerous.'

'No! It's not true.'

'I'm not lying. Didn't he ever hurt anyone when he was alive?' She closes her eyes, like she's shutting me out. 'Nan, please tell me. I'm scared. Scared of him.'

She sighs and opens her eyes again.

'He wasn't an angel, but he wouldn't do that, what you're saying.'

'Wouldn't he? So it's all right for me to go to the lake, is it? Nothing's going to happen? It's perfectly safe?'

And now she leans towards me and takes my hands in hers.

'Don't go down there, Nicola. Keep away.' She's looking into my eyes, and I see pain, fear and uncertainty in hers. She's scared too. 'Nicola,' she says again, 'promise me you won't go there. Promise.'

Her claw-like fingers are digging in, her eyes searching mine.

'Okay,' I say. 'I won't go. I'll head home in a bit. I got what I came for.'

Her hands relax a little, but she doesn't let go.

'Will I see you again?' she says.

Her eyes show genuine distress, and whatever I feel about her – and I'm really not sure what that is – I know that somehow we've made a sort of connection. A

246

connection I don't want to lose.

'Yes, of course. What's your number? I'll put it in my phone.'

'Ain't got one. I can't be doing with them. Phones bring bad news.'

'They bring good news too. If I got you one, we could text or something. Keep in touch.'

'I s'pose.'

'I'd like it if we did.'

She smiles. 'I'd like it too.'

I stay for a little while. She insists on giving me a couple of cans for my journey home. Our goodbyes are awkward. We don't hug or kiss – there's no physical contact at all, except right at the end when, as I'm turning away to go through the door, I think I feel her brush the top of my arm. As I glance back, her hand is hovering in mid-air, and she raises it and curls her fingers in an awkward, childish wave.

'Bye . . . Nan.'

'Oh God, call me Kerry. Nan's someone old, isn't it?'

I walk away thinking about her little claw-like hand, the lines puckering the edge of her mouth, the red threads clouding the whites of her eyes. And I think of how easy it was to lie to her.

Because, of course, I'm not heading home. I'm following the map on my phone – the one that shows the way from the flats to the park . . . and the lake.

THIRTY-TWO

The lake isn't like it was in the pictures. Seventeen years ago it was full to the banks, a grey stretch of water, rippling in the autumn wind. Fourteen years ago it was frozen over, transformed by ice. Now, just like the reservoir, the tide's gone out. The exposed mud that stretches away from the lip of the bank is cracked at the edges, like crazy paving.

I step down, away from my folded clothes and my bag, left together on the bank. The surface is hot, dry and solid. A large bird takes off from the far shore and flaps lazily towards me, scooping the air with its wings.

And suddenly I'm walking over ice, my feet crunching the thin layer of snow on top. The sun's in my eyes and it makes everything twinkle, like fairies live here – a sparkling, diamond world. I'm on my own here. I've left Nan behind with all the other people.

There's a funny noise, a squeaky, scrapey noise that makes my teeth feel funny. I look round to see if Nan's heard it and I'm falling, dropping down into a black hole. The cold takes my breath away. I open my mouth to shout and the black water rushes in.

I sink down, down, and it's so dark and so cold and I keep falling until I see the boy. He looks at me and smiles and says, 'Got you,' like this is some sort of game, except his voice doesn't sound like he's playing. There's something pretty in his hands – something shiny. He dangles it in front of my face.

'Do you like it?'

I stretch my hand out and he threads the chain through my fingers.

'You're mine now,' he says.

But there's someone else here too. Plunging into the water. Strong hands holding me under my arms, pushing me up towards the light . . .

The bird's grating cry brings me back to myself. The mud beneath my feet is radiating heat. I look around. The sun is dropping towards the top of the trees, shining in my eyes.

This is where it happened. Where Rob drowned, and where he found me beneath the ice. Kerry said she felt he was still here sometimes. Is he here now? At Turley, I felt nothing of him. No presence. Not a whisper. Here, a growing sense of dread is spreading through me.

I walk towards what little water remains in the centre of the space. As I get nearer, the mud changes consistency. My feet break the scabby surface and find the warm, soft, slippery ooze beneath. It squirts up between my toes and the sharp twang of decay hits my nostrils. Around me the mud is singing – hissing, bubbling, popping in the heat. The surface is alive as gas bubbles rise up, tiny creatures skating across. The back of my neck is burning in the sun. Flies buzz around my head. I swat them away, but they come back for more.

I pull one foot out of the mud. I'm wearing sticky grey socks now. I'm clothed in mud. As I step forward, my sole slips sideways. I flail my arms, trying to regain my balance, scared of falling. There's no one here to see, but it's not the embarrassment of slipping over I'm terrified of, it's the mud itself – the thought of it on my face. I gag a little, cough to clear my throat. I'm breathing hard, sweating freely.

I make myself walk on. The mud goes halfway up my calves and stops rising, thank God. I wade through towards the water, watching, listening, waiting. He must be here. He must be. I look around. There's no sign of him. I can hear kids' high-pitched voices drifting on the still air. An ice-cream van plays its off-key tune, weirdly distorted.

A shadow sweeps across the surface of the water. I look up. The sky is split in two overhead; one side is a clear, midsummer blue, the other is dark and dense, a solid bank of cloud boiling and churning within itself. I can't make sense of it – the sky has been clear for months on end. The cloud is like an alien ship, taking over the sky, casting its shadow on the earth.

In shade now, I've reached what's left of the lake water. A white, powdery scum sits on the surface. The grey mud seems inoffensive compared to this. A hot breeze ripples the water, making little waves, pushing it towards my legs. I step forward. The water's tepid. My foot sinks into the unseen mud below.

My mouth's dry. I swallow, gagging at the thought of the lake water in my throat. It's not going to happen, I tell myself – it can't be very deep, after all. The mud only shelved gently as I walked across it. I'll just wade in far enough so that I can see Rob. I won't get my face in this stinking, viscous stuff.

When I'm up to my waist, I turn round and look back at the shore. It seems a long way off. A picture comes into my head: Mum, Dad and Rob. Here. Seventeen years ago. Swimming, larking about, shouting, squealing, laughing. Before it all went wrong. Before Rob died. Before my dad . . . murdered him.

Did he, though? Two boys and a girl. Two brothers. What really went on?

He was a good boy deep down.

We did things . . . things I'm not proud of.

There's evil in the water.

He's back.

Suddenly I feel very, very alone. I should have brought someone with me. I shouldn't be here on my own.

'Yes, you should have brought them to me – Neisha and Carl.'

The light's playing tricks on me, light and shade dancing on the surface of the water, but now I can see him. Rob. Waist-high, like me, ten metres or so ahead.

'Rob.'

I can talk to him like this, with my head above the water.

He smiles. His eyes are disturbingly bright. He's zinging with energy.

'You found me,' he says.

'Yes.'

There's something deeply unsettling about him today. Anxiety stabs me under my ribs.

'Come in, Nic. Come deeper. You're not scared, are you?'

'No, I'm not scared.' But I am. Shivers of fear ripple up and down my spine.

'Don't lie to me. I know you, Nic.'

He's still some distance from me, but his voice is in my ear, inside my head. How's he doing that? I stand my ground, try to remember why I'm here.

'I need to talk to you,' I say.

He stops moving, and somehow that's worse than his restlessness.

'So talk.'

He's got the look he had in that school photo, the one in the news article, taken with Dad. He's kind of tipped his head back a bit, so he's looking down his nose at me. I'm not sure I can do this any more. But I'm here now, aren't I?

I take a deep breath.

'I want this to stop.'

He angles his head a little more.

'This? What do you mean, "this"?'

'The killing. The hurting.'

'I did it for you.'

'I didn't want it.'

'Didn't you?'

'No! I didn't want anyone hurt!'

'Yes, you did. Deep, deep down – you did.'

It's true, isn't it? Those feelings of resentment, of wanting to get my own back. But everyone has those. It's part of the mix of being human.

'What about all the other girls? The ones who died this summer?'

'I was looking for you. Process of elimination.'

'That's just sick.'

I start backing away. This was a mistake. Am I in too deep to save myself?

'Sick? Sick?' I didn't see him move, but he's in my face now. I flinch and keep trying to step backwards, but the mud seems to be holding me.

'Dad said I should stay away from water, and he was right. I'm leaving now. I shouldn't have come.'

'Dad? Carl?' He says his name like it's a dirty word, then he snorts, turns his head and spits. 'You don't want to believe anything he says, Nicola. He wouldn't know the truth if it bit him on the arse.'

'Why do you hate him?'

'Do you really want to know?' He seems even closer now and his voice – his voice is inside me.

'Yes,' I say.

'He murdered me, Nicola. Got rid of me so he could be with my girl.'

'Your girl,' I say. 'Neisha.'

'You worked it out,' he says. 'Yes. Neisha.'

'And you loved her?'

'Love. What's love?'

'You never loved me.'

253

Mum's voice! Here? I turn round and there she is, ten metres behind me, hand in hand with Dad.

'Mum? Dad?'

I'm laughing and crying at the same time, so relieved that they're here.

'He doesn't know the meaning of the word, Nic,' she says. 'Come here. Come here quickly.'

She holds her free arm out towards me, and it sends me back to the days when I was little, when I'd toddle away from her in the garden or the park or the shopping centre. She'd crouch down and hold her arms open wide, and she wouldn't have to say anything – it was the only signal I needed, and I'd run back and let myself be wrapped up in her embrace, feel her warmth, breathe her in. Safe and sound.

I try to move, but I'm stuck.

'No!' Rob shouts.

I look from him to Mum and back again. Above us, thunder is rolling around the sky. The mud beneath my feet seems to be dissolving. I'm sinking as I speak. I step to the left a little, find some solid ground . . . then that, too, seems to melt away.

'Have you hurt her, Rob? Have you put your hands on her?' Mum says. Beside her, Dad's arms are taut. I can see the tendons in his neck standing out like wire under the skin.

'Of course not. What do you think I am?'

He's moved in the water. Now he's between me and them. I feel cut off, like a connection's broken. I want my mum. I want my dad.

'I know what you are,' Mum says.

'I care about Nic,' Rob says.

'You don't care about anyone.'

Mum and Dad are shifting where they stand, too, trying to find their footing. Beneath us, the mud is turning into quicksand.

'I cared about *you* once,' Rob says.

'No. You hurt me. You tried to kill me. I was too young to handle it then. It's different now. I'm different. You're not hurting my daughter.'

Mum's voice is clear and strong. Her words carry the punch of a prize fighter.

Rob hurt her? He tried to kill her?

And then I hear Rob's voice.

'I won't hurt Nic, Neisha. Drowning doesn't hurt.'

A bolt of forked lightning snakes from the sky to the edge of the lake, followed immediately by a noise like the world is tearing down the middle. For a split second the faces behind me are bleached out, the water turns into a blinding mirror. I try to scream but it freezes in my throat.

There's nothing beneath my feet now, nothing to hold me up, and I sink up to my neck. Instinctively I paddle my arms and legs, treading water. I try to swallow my rising panic. I can swim, right? I can *really* swim, so this is all going to be okay.

I look across at Mum and Dad. They're in the water, too. I can see the whites of Mum's eyes as she jerks her face clear of the surface. She's terrified. Dad's thrashing his arms. He spits water out of his mouth. 'Nic, swim for the shore!' he shouts.

All we have to do is head for the edge. It's not that far. There's not much water, after all. But they're both wearing jeans and T-shirts. Sodden heavy cloth, dragging them down.

There's another flash and an explosion at the same time, and I'm hit, pushed through the water, all the breath knocked out of me. I'm blinded, blindsided. A piece of flotsam tossed and turned.

When everything stops moving and my eyes adjust, I'm under water. I can't see anyone else. I don't know which way is up, so I let my body work it out – feel it, sense the difference in light, the effect of gravity – then I flip round and head for the surface, breaking through, gulping air into my lungs.

I look round for the others.

I can see the back of Mum's head, a few metres away. I call out to her and she turns round. There's a vivid red mark down one side of her face, forked like a branch, as if a tree had just whipped her and left its imprint. Her eyes are wide and curiously dull. I don't think she can see me. I don't think she can see anything.

She's not swimming but she's moving away from me in the water, being carried off to my left in the current. Current? We're in a lake. Why is the water swirling like this? I can feel the power of it against my body. Mum's moving to the left, I'm being swept to the right. I don't understand.

Mum looks back at me. Her mouth opens and shuts, and then she disappears under the surface.

'Neisha!' Dad's seen her too. He's the other side of her,

and now he starts swimming towards the spot where she was – desperately grabbing at the water, kicking hard – but he's swimming against the current, being taken further away.

'No, Dad, let me!'

The water's carried me round now, so I'm getting nearer to where she disappeared. And now it clicks. The current is circular, like some sort of whirlpool. I swim a few strokes, going with the flow, then take a long deep breath and dive down.

It's difficult to see anything in this muddy, churned-up world. I force my eyes to stay open, twisting my head this way and that. I usually have to fight my body's natural desire to float when I'm swimming under water, but here the water feels like it's drawing me down. Something hits the side of my ribs. I flail my hands in the water, trying to push whatever it is away. Instead of the scrappy bark of a branch, my hand finds something delicate and fleshy. I'm holding someone's wrist. Without letting go, I move my other hand up the arm, then across the body to get a grip under their armpit. I turn the body so that I can see the face close to. It's Mum.

Her eyes are open and vacant. For a moment, I think she's gone, but suddenly there's a flicker of recognition in her face and she starts moving her arms and legs, almost as if she was climbing a ladder. Her hands are pushing me down. Her knees catch my legs and stomach. She'll kill us both if she carries on like this.

There's someone else here too. I look for Dad's face, hoping I'll be able to signal to him that he needs to help prise Mum off me and get her to the surface. I can't see him clearly, but my stomach tightens when I realise that the shape next to us in the water can't be Dad, in his navy T-shirt and jeans. It's too pale.

Rob's moving around us, like he used to move around me in the pool. Under and over, circling.

In the pool, at the beginning, it felt like we were dancing together. We were in tune with each other and the water. Here, it's different. Predatory. Menacing. A shark scenting blood.

And all the time, we're being drawn down, away from the surface, away from light and air and hope.

Mum's digging her fingers into my skin. I try to shake her off. No good. I let go of her with one hand to try to shoehorn her fingers away, but when I manage it, her loose hand thrashes out and finds my face, fingertips pulling at an eyelid, lodging in my nose and the corner of my mouth. She doesn't mean to, and I know that it's panic controlling her body, but she's doing Rob's work for him.

If she'd just let go, maybe I could save us both.

Let go, Rob says. *Let go of your breath, Nic. You don't need it any more.*

No!

It doesn't hurt. I promise. Relax and let it happen.

Mum's grip is losing its power. Can she hear him too? I don't want her to give up, but at least I've got a chance to help her now.

I jerk my head away from her and wriggle my shoulder from her grip. I turn her and move round in the water, so that she's got her back to me. She makes a half-hearted effort to resist, but the fight's pretty much gone out of her. I wedge my left arm under her armpit, tip her head back with my other hand, turn it and lean forward. I squeeze at the sides of her mouth to open her lips, then press my lips to hers and give her some of my air. Close to, her face is a blur, but I can see her eyes widen.

Don't give up. Let me help you. If only she could read my thoughts.

Rob can.

It's too late. I've got you. I've got you both.

I pull my head away and squash Mum's lips closed. Then I reach up high and pull the water towards me, kicking my feet as hard as I can. Mum's clothes are weighing us down. The water is pulling against me. But I won't give up. We turn together, revolving in the current. And I get it now. The water's draining away somehow. It's like going down a plughole. However hard I try to fight it, the forces are too strong.

I might stand a chance if I let go of Mum, tried to break away on my own. I might get out, but Mum wouldn't. She's stopped struggling now.

If I leave her, I won't see her again. Not alive.

If I stay, we'll both die.

I can't see a way out.

'Go, Nic. Leave me now. It's okay.'

It's her voice. I can hear it as clear as a bell. How can she be talking to me?

Mum? I stop trying to swim upwards and instead turn her to face me again.

A trickle of bubbles escapes from between her lips. Her

259

eyes are open, unblinking. Can she see me?

'It's time to go. It's okay. I love you.'

Her mouth doesn't move, so where's the voice coming from?

I search her face for signs of life. My own oxygen is running out – I know the feeling from swimming lengths under water. You hold on, fighting the urge to surface, clamping your mouth shut to get one more stroke, a few more metres, and your body seems to be on autopilot, and for a few moments the aching doesn't seem real any more – you could do this for ever. It's a dangerous thing, your body playing tricks on you. Because if you don't make the effort to breathe now, it can be too late. Everything shuts down.

I haven't got much oxygen, but what I've got I can share with her.

I put my mouth on hers again, make a seal round our lips with my fingers, try to force the air from inside me into her. It's like kissing a dummy. She's as unresponsive as the nightmarish orange torso that sank to the bottom of the swimming pool, waiting to be rescued.

Too late. She's mine. Rob's next to us, his face hideously close. *And so are you.*

The air that I tried to give Mum rises away from us.

'*Leave her alone.*' Mum's voice again.

I look around. She's the other side of me, her face near mine, opposite Rob. But she's still in front of me, too. What's going on? How can she be in two places at once?

We swirl in the current, the four of us together, round and around.

260

No. It's not enough.

'*Let her live, Rob. She's our daughter.*'

And it feels like the world stops turning, even though we're still circling on our sickening water ride.

Rob's my dad?

She's mine?

'*Yes. Let her live. Let her have the life she deserves.*'

I look through the murk into the eyes of a seventeen-year-old boy. My father.

Nicola, he says.

'*Let her go, Rob. You've got me now.*'

It's not enough.

'*It's what you wanted all this time. You've won, Rob. It's over. But you can't have our daughter. She's got her whole life to live.*'

Something bullets towards us through the water, a dark mass coming from above. There's no time to get out of the way. It knocks into me and Mum, skittling us away from each other. The momentum carries me through the water and I find myself rising, drifting. I've been thrown off the merry-go-round, and I break the surface and gasp, my aching chest heaving as I take in air. There's another flash of lightning, and thunder fills my ears. I scull my hands in the water and look frantically around. The lake seems smaller, the flat field of mud around it bigger.

Someone surfaces nearby.

'Nic, is that you?' Dad shouts. He's frantic, wild-eyed, exhausted. 'I'm going back for Mum!'

'No, I will! I'll do it, Dad!'

But before I can dive, there's another crack of thunder and I'm drawn down again, feet first, but this time they hit something solid. The water keeps dragging against me, draining away. My body is heavy out of the water, my legs collapse under me, and I'm sitting on a blanket of wet mud, watching the remains of the lake pour into a hole a few metres away. Dad's sprawled on his back, like a landed fish. I crawl over to him on my hands and knees, slithering on the grey slime.

'Dad! Dad, are you okay?'

I help him sit up.

'What the—? Where's Neisha?'

We both look at the scene in front of us.

The last of the water tips over the edge of the hole. All around us is damp, dark mud. There's debris scattered about: an old supermarket trolley, some shoes, a traffic cone.

I can't see Mum anywhere.

We both have the same thought at the same time.

'She must be—'

We scramble to the edge of the sinkhole. It's too dark to see anything. Too deep to see the bottom.

'I'm going in,' Dad says. He starts peeling off his T-shirt.

I take hold of his arm.

'You can't. You don't know how deep it is. Please, Dad, don't. Besides—'

'What?'

'I think it's . . . I think she's already . . .'

I can't say it, but he knows anyway. He freezes, with his shirt halfway up his back.

'Did you see her? Were you with her?'

I nod. If I try and speak now, the grief that's knotted in my throat will escape.

'But it was dark down there, you wouldn't be able to tell . . .' He yanks his shirt over his head, drops it in the mud, stands up and starts undoing the buttons on his jeans.

'She spoke to me, Dad.' My words are blurred by tears, but he hears them and he stops again.

'She spoke to you. Underwater.'

He doesn't call me crazy or tell me off for making it up. He slowly sinks back into the mud next to me, and takes my hands in his.

'What did she say?'

'That he should let me go. That she loved me.'

That I was Rob's daughter.

Dad's shoulders sag.

'Rob. He's got her now. He got her in the end.'

'I'm sorry. I tried . . . I tried so hard . . .'

The rest is lost in tears. Nothing can hold them back now. And Dad cries too. We move closer and hold each other. And as the thunder fades into the distance, the rain starts. A few drops to begin with – on the top of my head, the back of my neck, and my arms – then more and more until my sobs are drowned out by the noise of the rain hammering into mud.

THIRTY-THREE

Kingsleigh cemetery is a peaceful place. It's on the edge of the town, in a dip with water meadows beyond its low flint walls. You can hear the steady hum of traffic from the bypass and the chatter of birds. We've walked here from the B&B and now we stand together inside the gates, looking across at a sea of gravestones.

'He's over there, if you want to . . . visit. There's a little plaque set in the ground. I'll take you if you want . . .' Dad nods towards a neatly tended section, more like a public park than anything else.

'Is that why we've come here?'

'No. No, we've come to see Harry and Iris.'

I've got my arm linked in his and he leads me down narrow paths to a leafy corner. He stops in front of an untended grave. The headstone sits squarely at one end.

Iris Hemmings, died 25th June, 2013, aged 76.

Lower down another name has been added.

And Harry Hemmings . . . Reunited at last.

'I don't understand,' I say. 'Who are they – *were* they?'

'Have you got the necklace?'

'Yeah, you already asked that before we set off, remember? Look. Here it is.'

I haven't been able to wear it – it just seems wrong. I've been keeping it in my pocket. I've taken it out from time to time, opened it up and looked at the photo. Mum and Rob. Together. My mum and dad. The words jar in my head. They sound wrong, like fingernails scraping on a blackboard. Is it true? Was it just something Mum said to try and save me?

I take the locket out of my pocket now.

'This is where it belongs,' Dad says. 'It was Iris's first. I think she should have it back.'

'I still don't get it. Did she give it to Mum?'

He sighs, then presses his lips together.

'Dad?'

'It's a long story.'

'Shall we sit down?' There's a bench nearby, lodged comfortably under the umbrella-spoke branches of a tree. We walk over and sit side by side, looking back towards the grave.

'Iris Hemmings was a good person, a kind person. When I was at school I did some work for her and her husband, Harry – a bit of gardening, painting, that sort of thing. They were a smashing couple. She'd make me lemon squash and sponge cake. He let me borrow some of his books. He gave me a copy of one I needed for school.'

'That's lovely. Bit like grandparents.'

'Yeah. That's it, Nic. That's just how it was.'

'So?'

He sighs again, then starts talking, keeping his eyes fixed on the ground, his voice soft and low.

'We broke into their house. Me and Rob. I thought it was empty. It wasn't. Iris was home on her own. Well, her and her dog. Rob . . . Rob kicked the dog. Killed it. Then he took the necklace from round Iris's neck, even though she begged him not to. We were in the backyard when she found the dog on the kitchen floor. She collapsed and we just . . . we just left her.'

I can't think of anything to say. Dad's closed his eyes. His lips are still moving, but he's not making any sound.

'Dad?'

He opens his eyes, but is careful to avoid mine.

'She died. That night. Everyone thought it was just the shock of her finding the dog. No one knew about me and Rob, except Harry. He knew the necklace was missing, knew someone had been in there. He tried to tell people, but they didn't listen to him. We killed her, Nic. As good as. Rob gave the locket to Neisha a week or so later.'

'But they found it with me when I fell in the lake when I was little. That's what Kerry said. That's what it said on the envelope.'

'Your mum was wearing it the day Rob died. It must

266

have come off.' He falters, then runs both hands over his scalp, like he's trying to squeeze the thoughts out. 'God, I can't lie to you any more. He took it back from her, ripped it off her neck in the lake. He had it – he must have dropped it when he . . . when he drowned.'

'They were fighting?'

'No. He was hurting her. He attacked her. So I jumped in, tried to stop him.'

He's telling me the truth now, so I don't see that I have a choice. I've got to do the same.

'He told me it was murder.'

Dad sits up and turns to face me.

'That's not right, Nic. It was an accident. We were fighting, but he was okay. His feet got caught in some weed, that's what killed him.'

'He never believed that. He was out for revenge. I didn't know . . . when I saw him the first few times, he helped me. I thought he was . . . I thought he was my friend.'

His face becomes slack, as my words sink in.

'All that time I was trying to protect you, keep you safe. He was there.'

'Yes. I didn't know he was my . . . never suspected he was my . . .' Dad? Uncle? 'Not until Milton and I did a bit of digging. I found my birth certificate with the different names, and Milton found all your forum posts and the article about him – Rob – drowning. It was like different pieces of a jigsaw. I'm still not sure how they all fit together.'

'He could have taken you at any time . . .'

'But he didn't. Like I said, he was my friend . . .'

'. . . while he was killing all those other girls.'

'I know. You were right. All those girls. It was him.'

The horror of it is still raw. Rob. The serial killer. My friend. My uncle. My dad?

'It feels like my fault.'

'No, Nic. None of this, none of it, is your fault. That's what they do – bullies, abusers, torturers – they make you think that you're to blame, that you made it happen. That's just wrong.'

'Is it over? Will it ever be over?'

'Do you still see him?'

'No. Not since that day . . . This'll sound stupid, but I think maybe Mum sorted him out. The last time I saw her, underwater, she had such . . . strength. God, Dad, I miss her. I wish I could see her again.'

'She's still with you. And me. Always will be. We loved her and she loved us. That doesn't just go away.'

I wish it was true. I wish things didn't just stop when someone dies. But all I've got now, filling every waking moment, is her absence. The space she used to occupy. The silence where her voice should be. The utter loneliness of knowing that I'll never feel her arms round me again.

'So, the locket,' Dad says. 'Should we leave it here? Give it back to Iris?'

'Yes,' I say. 'I'd like that.'

We link arms again and walk back to the grave.

'How do we—? I mean, if we just leave it, someone will take it, won't they?'

'I've come prepared.' He digs into his rucksack and

brings out a little garden trowel.

'Blimey, Dad, you weren't kidding, were you?'

'And these, too.' He fishes out a paper bag, full of big, round, crispy-looking brown things.

'Onions? What the—?'

'Not onions, you dafty, bulbs. Daffodils. They'll come through in the spring.'

We kneel down either side of the rectangle of grass. Dad digs a sort of trench across it, not far from the headstone. I place the locket on the bare soil in the middle. Then I pick it up again.

'It's still got a picture in. I don't think it's right.'

I turn away a little from Dad, and prise the locket open with my thumbnail, then I pull the inner frame out and pick out the photo. I don't know what to do with it next, so stuff the tiny scrap of paper in my pocket.

'It's okay,' Dad says. 'I know, you know.'

'What?'

I snap the locket shut.

'I know about that picture. I know that Rob was your father.'

My turn to go slack-jawed.

'Seriously? Like, how long have you known?'

'Always. Since your mum told me she was pregnant.'

'You knew.'

'It didn't change anything. Not for me. I loved her. I knew I would love her child. And I did. Do. Always will.'

He's not smiling. He hasn't smiled since 'it' happened. His face is so serious, so tender, that I just want to hug him. But there's half a metre of human remains between us. It doesn't feel right. There'll be time for that later.

'It doesn't change anything for me either. You're my dad. You always will be.'

He doesn't smile, but there's a suggestion of one, a reminder of what his face looks like when he does smile.

'So,' he says, 'do you want to do the honours?'

I nod.

I put the locket back in the bottom of the trench and line the bulbs up from one side to the other.

'Okay?'

'Yeah.'

Dad covers everything up with loose soil until all I can see is a patch of fresh earth in a sea of grass. I sit back on my heels and admire our work.

'I'd like somewhere like this for Mum,' I say. Her body was recovered from the sinkhole by divers the day after she drowned.

'Yes, not here, though. Somewhere back home, so it's easy to visit her. They should release her body soon, then I'll sort it out. Maybe she could have Misty's ashes with her too.'

'Yeah, she'd like that. I'll help you, Dad. Help you sort it all out. Make sure we do it properly.'

'I know you will.'

'I love you, Dad.'

'I know. I love you, too.'

THREE MONTHS LATER

I stand with my toes curled over the edge of the block. The noise around me is almost deafening. The voice on the tannoy system announces each of us in turn and the crowd claps, shouts and whistles its approval – all of it echoing off the walls and ceiling, distorting and blurring at the edges.

I'm in lane five. When my name is read out, I look up to the stand.

Dad's there. He's got his camera at the ready to take pictures, but he's not looking at me through a lens right now. He's on his feet cheering and waving. Milton's mum is next to him. She's sitting down but she's got both hands in the air, like a worshipper in a revivalist church. She and Milton have been coming to all my competitions. They do a proper job – bring cushions to make the plastic seats more bearable and a big cool-bag full of sandwiches, drinks and snacks. Mrs Adeyemi wasn't there the day we got home from Kingsleigh, but she'd been in our house and stocked up our fridge. Mum had called round to hers to leave her a key before she and Dad chased after me.

'She said it was just in case, but why after all this time? When she left she hugged me, like she was saying goodbye. When I heard the news I knew that she'd been trying to tell me something. And I knew I couldn't sit on my big behind in that chair any longer. She was counting on me.'

Milton's the other side of his mum. He's taken over from Dad as my statistician. He'll have today's time and placing on his database before I've even got changed. But he won't give me a bollocking if it all goes wrong. Neither will Dad.

'Whatever happens today, I want you to know that I'm proud of you,' Dad says. 'And I know Mum is, too.'

Mum. She should be there, sitting next to Dad. Don't think about it. Don't lose it now.

I give everyone a quick wave and then try to blank it all out. I use my rituals to calm my nerves and focus: check my hair is tucked into my hat, adjust my goggles, look ahead at the turquoise rectangle of water.

The starting judge tells us to get ready. The hubbub starts to die down.

I take a couple of long, smooth breaths.

I can do this. I know I can.

I'm going to do it for Dad, and Milton and his mum, who've stood by me, got me through the last few months.

And I'm going to do it for Mum.

'Ready.'

I wait for the electronic tone, desperate not to go too quickly. And then it's there, and I sense the others starting to move, and I spring away from the block. All I've got in my mind now is the shape of a perfect dive. I cut through the water and start flexing my stomach muscles, dolphining down and along as far as I can, my ears full of the sound of rushing water.

I make the surface, turn to the side, breathe in and roll back again, reaching forward, kicking hard. I find my rhythm quickly and settle into it. I don't try to check where the others are. It doesn't matter. I'm going to swim my best, and this is going to be the best swim of my life.

I'm on the last lap when I hear a voice.

I'm with you, Nic. I'm here, my beautiful girl.

I look left and right, trying to see where it's coming from.

Keep going. Don't stop now.

I stretch a little further, kick a little harder. The water buoys me up, gives me strength. I feel part of it. We're one and the same.

The change in tiles marks five metres from home. I want to take a breath, but I don't want to lose any time. I push on, sprinting faster, pushing myself, reaching forward and slamming my fingers into the wall. Still underwater, I look around at the thrashing arms and legs, but I can't see what I'm looking for.

Where are you?

Ssh, Mum says. I'm here, Nic. I'm right beside you. I wouldn't miss this for the world.

Acknowledgements

I'd like to thank:

Barry, Imogen, Elinor, Rachel and everyone else at my amazing publisher, Chicken House.

My foreign publishers and translators, especially dear Anja, Uwe-Michael, Dorothy and Laszlo.

The booksellers, librarians, English teachers and bloggers who champion my books. I owe you so much.

And lastly, but especially dear to me, my readers, particularly the ones who write, email or tweet and tell me what they think. You'll never know how much your messages have meant to me.

ALSO BY RACHEL WARD

NUMBERS
Rachel Ward

Since the day her mother died, Jem has known about the numbers. When she looks in someone's eyes, she can see the date they will die.

Life is hard, until she meets a boy called Spider. Suddenly her world seems brighter.

But on a trip to London, Jem foresees a chain of events that will shatter their lives for ever ...

... intelligent and life-affirming.
PHILIP ARDAGH, GUARDIAN

... utterly compelling.
SUNDAY TELEGRAPH

Paperback, ISBN 978-1-905294-93-0, £6.99
ebook, ISBN 978-1-908435-02-6, £6.99

ALSO AVAILABLE:

NUMBERS 2: THE CHAOS
Paperback, ISBN 978-1-906427-30-6, £6.99
ebook, ISBN 978-1-908435-04-0, £6.99

NUMBERS 3: INFINITY
Paperback, ISBN 978-1-906427-66-5, £6.99
ebook, ISBN 978-1-908435-06-4, £6.99

 Find out more about Chicken House books and authors.
Visit our website: www.doublecluck.com

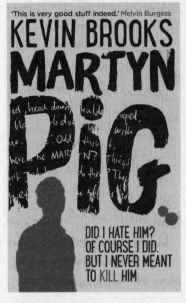

'This is very good stuff indeed.' Melvin Burgess

KEVIN BROOKS

MARTYN PIG

DID I HATE HIM?
OF COURSE I DID.
BUT I NEVER MEANT
TO KILL HIM

MARTYN PIG
Kevin Brooks

Did I hate him? Of course I hated him. But I never meant to kill him.

With his father dead, Martyn has a choice. Tell the police what happened – and be suspected of murder. Or get rid of the body and get on with the rest of his life.

Simple, right? Not quite. One story leads to another. Secrets and lies become darker and crazier. And Martyn is faced with twists and turns that leave him reeling.

Life is never easy. But death is even harder.

. . . will keep you gripped.
OBSERVER

In a word, genius!
WATERSTONES

. . . a cult novel.
INDEPENDENT

Paperback, ISBN 978-1-910002-00-1, £7.99
ebook, ISBN 978-1-908435-71-2, £7.99

 Find out more about Chicken House books and authors.
Visit our website: www.doublecluck.com